SECRETS OF THE REAPERS

THE REAPER CHRONICLES

BOOK THREE

SARAH McKNIGHT

For my husband, Alan, who hated the ending of Book 2 so much, he convinced me to change my plans. I think it was worth it. I hope you do, too.

SECRETS OF THE REAPERS

REAPER #1632

The man sits on the edge of the sagging mattress, his handgun balancing precariously atop his knee. One might think the careless gesture dangerous, should the weapon slip and fall to the ground, but I suppose in his current state of mind, an accident may be a blessing.

We have been talking for hours, Steven Kelton and I. A fascinating man. Human, but not quite. Not anymore. And faced with an impossible choice. Everything hangs here in this dim and dusty motel room, stagnant. It's as if the world itself has stopped turning. But I know that is not the case.

Assignments are waiting for me, and I can't get to them until I cross this one off my list.

"You're really sure?" Steve asks, and he raises his weapon to study the glossy texture.

"Of course not. I can't be sure of anything."

"And if it doesn't work?" Steve continues. His finger brushes the trigger, and a frown is set deep into his mouth.

I can only shrug helplessly, the bones of my shoulders raising the black fabric of my robe.

He chuckles, but there is no humor in the sentiment. "That's reassuring."

"Death isn't meant to be reassuring. It simply is."

It's almost funny that this man, who has already died once, fears the prospect of death so much. He should understand it better than any human alive.

A rush of air escapes between his lips, and he runs a hand through his silver-streaked hair, which has gone spiky with so many repeats of the same gesture. "If it doesn't work, you promise you'll—"

"I already said I would try." An odd sensation is creeping into the hollow space beneath my ribs. It takes a moment for me to recognize it as a rising panic. I can't recall ever feeling anything like this before.

At least, not since I've been like this. I almost welcome it. "Now, get on with it."

He doesn't like my demand. I can tell by the way his tightened lips twist downward and his thumb twitches over the gun's safety. "I'm trusting you to pull this off."

"One step at a time," I tell him. Then, as an afterthought, "It will hurt." Though the concept of pain has long since been lost on me, I feel I must warn him. Humans are such fragile creatures, terrified of the stretching unknown. Knowing something as simple as the coming onset of pain somehow eases their minds, at least a little bit. I certainly don't understand it. I don't think I ever did.

Steve takes in a long breath, as if to steady himself, to build up for what's to come. "Good luck," he tells me as he raises the weapon.

"To you, as well."

I turn my back, allowing a private moment. The whipcrack of the shot is loud, even to me. Something heavy hits the worn carpet with a thump. I let my jaw fall open and pretend to take in my own steadying breath before turning back around and setting to work.

Reaper HQ is teeming with more activity than usual as war breaks out and more lives are lost. A Reaper's job is never done. I know there are assignments waiting on my desk, but the Big Boss has demanded to see me in private after dealing with the Steven Kelton situation, and I cannot keep him waiting.

The guards outside the Big Boss's office nod as I approach the grand mahogany doors, carved with intricate patterns and ancient symbols that have lost their meaning over the millennia. They push open the doors and allow me to enter. For the first time, I wonder if they would be heavy to someone who had muscles and nerves. Despite our lack of these once human features and our supernatural qualities, the task does not seem easy.

The office has been cleared of any additional guards, likely in preparation for my arrival. If word got out about Mr. Kelton and his unprecedented cycle from human, to Reaper, to human once more, all hell would break loose. That is, if this place isn't already hell. Sometimes, I wonder.

I push those thoughts aside as I stroll down the black marble-tiled hall, passing rows upon rows of white columns and iron sconces flickering with eternal flames. The Big Boss sits upon his plush velvet throne, its golden molding sparkling in the firelight. The deep-set embers in his eyes burn fiercely hot as I come to a stop before him.

The moment of truth has arrived. I find myself wishing I had my scythe to cling to – anything to distract me from his menacing glare. But it is stowed away in my locker until it's time for me to embark on my next assignment. I let my arms hang at my sides.

"I see the nuisance's wick has been cut," the Big Boss says, and his gravelly voice grates at me in a way it never has before.

"Yes, he's taken care of."

"Excellent." Although his face is nothing more than a yellowed skull, cracked and beginning to crumble with age, I sense the fear he had been carrying dissolving, and my theory has been proven correct. "I trust you will not mention a word of this. To anyone."

"Of course," I assure my boss. And this, I do mean. Steven Kelton, once a Reaper, found a way to become human again. I shudder to think what would happen if the thousands of other Reapers toiling away at Headquarters, taking lives day in and day out, discovered that there was, somehow, some way, a real way out. But for all the Big Boss and I know, this whole thing was nothing but a fluke. Either way, the Big Boss would likely have a riot to contend with, and that would spell trouble for everyone.

He seems to be sizing me up, and I feel myself shrinking under his already massive form. My vision darts to his scythe, proudly hung on the wall behind his throne. It is more ancient than he is; the blade rumored to be crafted from the meteorite that caused life to burst forth upon the earth and the petrified handle from the first tree to stretch upward to the sky. It is rarely used these days, but when it is, Reapers who are about to lose their heads always quake before its awesome power. I do not intend to be on the receiving end of that blade.

"The matter is settled then," the Big Boss declares, his finger-bones gripping the carved arms of his throne. "Return to your duties, Reaper #1632, and we will both put this incident behind us. For good."

"Yes, sir."

Another strange feeling overcomes my skeletal frame as I return to my desk, and after a moment of silent contemplation, I am able to pinpoint it for what it is: relief. The sensation is almost enough to fill me with joy – a concept I am well aware of but have no first-hand experience. I relish it, and for the first time since coming to as a new recruit, I have something I truly want to pursue.

Just thinking about these things is putting me in danger, but now that I've started, I can't seem to stop.

I keep my skull bent down, my gaze on the worn marble floor, as I wind through the maze of thousands of identical cubicles. I know the way to my desk by heart. I am coming up on a big milestone around HQ – a full century as a Reaper. And with a spotless record, a celebration is sure to be had in my honor. The centennial anniversary is usually awarded with the gift of a particularly large assignment, typically just to show off the skills the celebrated Reaper has attained during their time as a ruthless death machine. With all the war breaking out, I haven't given much thought as to what my special assignment will be. I doubt I will be surprised.

Finally reaching my desk, I find the polished wood scattered with sealed envelopes. Within each envelope will be a single sheet of paper neatly printed with a name and location. Assigned Deaths are usually made up of the old and the sick, with an occasional accident thrown in for fun. There's not much room for creativity when assigned to take out an elderly woman sleeping peacefully in her bed, or a middle-aged man so loaded up with painkillers that he no longer remembers he is alive in the first place. But I've already completed my quota for the month, and these assignments are all I have. Business as usual must resume.

I tear open the first envelope and get to work.

STEVE

Beep...beep...beep...

Not too long ago, I was pulled out of a groggy sleep by the same damn sound, only this time, it doesn't come as a shock. I'm still surprised, sure, because the cynical part of me didn't expect this to actually work. But here I am, in another hospital, hooked up to machines that assure me I'm still very much alive. I want to laugh, but I'm either too doped up or still too sleep-weary to push air over my vocal cords.

Darkness clouds my vision, and I realize it's because my eyes are still closed. They must have given me some good stuff. A pleasant sense of detachment fogs my mind as I force my heavy eyelids to open. It takes a while, but after several exhausting minutes, I'm staring at a white-tiled ceiling marred with yellowed water stains. Yikes. Hope that doesn't speak to the quality of this facility.

I pull in a slow, careful breath, and a distant pain blooms in my right shoulder. Makes sense. A bullet went through it. But I welcome the pain. It only serves to confirm that I am still alive.

"Take that, you bastard," I croak, and manage a hollow cackle. My tongue sits heavy in my mouth, dry as a bone and desperate for water. With great effort, I turn my head to the left and find a door standing partially open. Shadows pass, and the unmistakable clicking of heels on linoleum echo down the hall.

"Nurse," I whisper, then clear my throat and try again. "Nurse!"

The door opens, and a young blonde in a white cap pokes her head in. Her mouth broadens into a perfectly straight, white smile. "Mr. Kelton, you're awake! I'll get the doctor." She scurries off before I can say anything else.

Chuckling softly, I turn my head back and look up at the ceiling again. I sure am awake. The fuzziness of sleep is lifting, and though my return to consciousness brings with it an onslaught of bright pain radiating from my shoulder, I couldn't possibly care less. I'm alive. So far, so good. Step one is complete.

A young man in a white coat steps into the room, the blonde nurse at his heels. He checks the machines at my bedside as he speaks.

"You gave us quite a scare, Mr. Kelton. You lost a lot of blood."

"I'm sure I did," I agree, and his brows furrow, likely due to my unusual reaction. *Act natural...*

The doctor frowns. "The gunshot wound you suffered, well, it appeared to be self-inflicted."

"It was." My teeth grind together. *Act* more *natural.*

Doctor and nurse exchange a worried look, and I realize I may still get myself committed after all. While I do have some time to spare, that would throw a serious wrench in my plans. I clear my throat and put on my best somber expression while the nurse cranks up the head of my bed so I can sit up.

"I'm afraid I was going through quite the rough patch," I explain in a voice filled with sorrow. It's not exactly a lie. "You see, my company was nearly ruined thanks to a backstabbing partner, and then my girlfriend passed away in a terrible car accident. I suppose it was all just too much to bear. But I've seen the light now," I declare, forcing a sense of triumph into my tone.

They look at each other again, as if they're having a telepathic conversation. I would very much like to be in on it.

"That certainly sounds like a lot to go through," the doctor says, choosing each word carefully. The nurse nods along in sympathy. "You were very lucky that you missed any major arteries. The bullet went cleanly through your shoulder."

"That is lucky," I agree of my completely intentional injury.

"But I'm afraid you may have some permanent nerve damage." The doctor lowers his gaze as he delivers the news, flipping through the papers on his clipboard as he speaks. "You may not regain full function of your right arm. I'm going to have a physical therapist come in to speak with you about next steps once your wound heals. I'm going to have our psychologist come to chat with you as well." He lifts his gaze and studies my face for some sort of reaction. I settle on tight lips and a wrinkled brow. In reality, a bum arm is a small price to pay for what I'm planning to do next.

"That sounds good," I say, only because he's expecting me to say something. "Thanks for keeping me alive. I appreciate it."

The doctor clears his throat and the nurse's smile looks more and more forced by the minute.

"Yes, well, you are very lucky, Mr. Kelton," he repeats. After a pause, he continues, "Your driver's license says you're from Indiana. How exactly did you end up here in East Moline?"

East Moline! I had no idea my aimless drive took me all the way to Illinois. I shrug with my good shoulder.

"Like I said, I was going through something."

The doctor gives a curt nod and scribbles something down. "Do you have any family here? Friends?"

I shake my head.

"I see. Is there anyone we can call?"

Well, let's see… Susan's dead, everyone at my company thinks I've lost my goddamn mind, my uptight sister is the last person I want to talk to, and my only friend is an otherworldly Grim Reaper only I can see. So, I shake my head again.

The sympathetic look is back on the nurse's face. "No one at all, Mr. Kelton?"

I give her a reassuring smile. "Don't worry, sweetheart, I'm alright."

The doctor doesn't seem to care much for that answer, but he sighs and lets the subject drop. "Your vitals are looking good. I'd like to keep you here for a few days for observation."

Translation: He wants to make sure I'm not going to try to off myself again.

"That's fine with me," I say, hoping that the more agreeable I am, the quicker they'll let me go. I'm itching to move on to phase two of the Big Plan #1632 and I spent so many hours concocting.

Seemingly satisfied, the nurse and doctor leave the room to tend to other patients in need of much more care than me. The sudden emptiness is unsettling. I wiggle my foot with impatience and sip on water from the pitcher beside my bed while I wait for my next guest.

The hospital's physical therapist is a woman about my own age with jet black hair streaked with thick gray highlights. I like them. It makes her seem like she's dealt with her fair share of tough patients, and she knows just how to stick it to them. She's brisk and to the point, which I also like.

After a brief demonstration of a few simple exercises for me to begin once my shoulder heals, she tells me she's going to compile a list of physical therapists in my hometown and makes me promise to set up an appointment with one of them. She looks at me with scrutiny when I assure her I'll do just that. Years of working in patient care must have instilled her with a pretty spot-on lie detector. But she has no choice but to take my word, and she leaves the room with a briskness that shows she means nothing but business.

The psychologist is another story. Young, and probably eager to become the next Carl Jung or some other great, he spends an agonizingly long time at my bedside asking questions in a soft, practiced tone and forcing me to look deep into his blank blue eyes as I answer.

He wants to know how I ended up in the hospital today.

"I shot myself," I say with a bluntness that seems to unsettle him for the briefest of moments.

"I heard," he says, his expression a somber mirror of what he probably expects me to convey. "And what do you believe led you to that point?"

I give him the same spiel. Stanley's betrayal. Susan's horrific death. Good enough reasons for anyone to crack. I leave out the part about #1632 and my own stint as a Grim Reaper, though. I'm really not trying to get myself committed. Not after coming this far.

"But I realized I have other reasons to live," I say in conclusion so I can get this guy off my case. I take a deep breath and really lay it on thick. "As soon as I pulled the trigger, I regretted it. I didn't actually want to die. After I took my sabbatical, I began taking various courses at the community center and realized I have a knack for creative writing. Susan, she encouraged me. Said I could actually do something with it. I realized I couldn't see her again by dying. But I could keep her spirit alive in the writing she wanted me to pursue. And so, now that I've been given this second chance, that's exactly what I'm going to do."

I dare a glance at the psychologist's face and find he's eating this shit up. Excellent.

"That would be a beautiful way to immortalize her," he says like the sap he is.

I nod and, for added effect, give his wrist a squeeze along with my most earnest gaze. "I have new goals now, new things to live for, and I intend to pursue them."

This part isn't a lie, but if I explain my true intentions, I'll be committed faster than I can say "I'm cuckoo for Cocoa Puffs."

"I'm so glad you've discovered new meaning for your life, especially after all the hardships you've suffered in such a short amount of time," he says, and I notice actual tears budding in the corners of his eyes. I fight to keep my own eyes from rolling as he continues, "But I would like for you to continue speaking with someone when you return home. At least for a little while. Is that something you can agree to, Mr. Kelton?"

"Yeah, absolutely," I say with enough enthusiasm to get him off my back. I think of poor Dr. Malcolm, who I probably terrified with my cryptic words at our last session, but I can't go back to him. I'd have to explain too much. I don't intend to see any other shrink anyway. My mind is perfectly clear now.

"Wonderful." The good psychologist smiles at my lies and stands. "I'll get a list together for you."

"Thank you, I really appreciate it." I smile, but not too brightly. Can't have him thinking I'm still teetering on the edge. "And thanks for the chat. It helped a lot."

He beams with so much pride it's almost blinding. "That's why I entered this field, Mr. Kelton. I'll be back soon."

I wave him off, and as soon as the room is empty again, an unnerving, rhythmic clacking noise erupts in the corner. Turning my head, I find #1632 standing in the shadows and clapping the bones of his hands together in a grotesque ovation.

"Good show, good show!" he says, bending at the waist in a bow as if he were the one performing.

I chuckle and settle back against the pillows, a sense of relief flooding my weary body at the sight of my new friend. "I take it since your skull is still attached to your spine, your theory was correct."

#1632 steps away from the corner and comes up to my bedside. He settles into the salmon pink leather chair the psychologist had just occupied and drapes his hands politely over his knees. "It seems the Big Boss is not nearly as omniscient as he wants us to believe."

"He really thinks I'm dead?"

"He knows I cut your wick, just as I was assigned to do. To him, and every other Reaper, that means you're dead and no longer a threat. The matter has been dropped."

I wave my hand over my head, as if feeling for that invisible, life-determining wick all Reapers have the privilege of seeing. "How much did you take off, by the way?"

"A few inches." He shifts in the chair like its uncomfortable against his nerveless ass. "To my knowledge, no one has ever tried this before. I have no idea how many years of your remaining life I removed."

"I don't care, as long as it's enough to get me to Heather."

Heather. The reason for my second chance. The reason for this whole plan. Heather, who was condemned to a life of being able to see the Grim Reapers after a near fatal car accident as a child. Heather, who lived in constant fear until she befriended me and saved me from an eternity of misery. Now, I return the favor. I know

I can do it, because the accident that damned her for life hasn't happened yet. She hasn't even been born.

My eyes drift to the calendar hanging by the bathroom door. 1979.

Shaking my head slowly, I turn back to #1632. "Twenty years. You and I have a very long wait, my friend."

#1632 holds out his hands, spreading his fingerbones in a gesture of resignation. "I have all eternity." Standing, he studies my face with his blank, hollow eyes. Deep inside the blackness, something flickers. "I'll check in when I can."

"Reaper #2007. Don't forget. He can be trusted."

He's quiet for a long time. "I sincerely hope this plan works, Steven Kelton. For the both of us."

I smile, but it's tight as all the ways this could go wrong swirl in my mind. "You and me both."

REAPER #2311

Around and around we go.

The thought dissipates from my mind as quickly as it comes, and I am left with nothing but a hollowness as I stare at gleaming white fingerbones that bend and curl when I tell them to, confirming they belong to me. This is who I am.

The bench I'm sitting on should be hard, but I feel nothing. Maybe I should be cold, or hot. But no sense of temperature seeps into my bones. A billowy black robe covers my legs, and I study the ninety-degree angle at which my knees are bent beneath the fabric. Upon closer inspection, I find numbers stitched near my left shoulder in red thread: 2311. Below the numbers, a sticker with the word *Trainee*.

I'm alone in this small, gray-tiled waiting room. I get the sense that this is not always the case.

A latch clicks somewhere, and the metal door is pulled open, revealing a black-cloaked Grim Reaper, straight out of all those medieval paintings, holding a clipboard to their chest. I should be terrified by this thing walking briskly over to me, but I feel nothing. The hollowness within me sucks up any potential emotion before I can fully register it, like a black hole.

"Reaper #2311." The voice that comes out of the Reaper's skull is high-pitched and nasally, and she pulls her clipboard back to reveal the number stitched into her own robe: 986. I feel like I should stand, so I do, and she continues. "Welcome to Reaper Headquarters. You are here because you committed the act of murder at least once in your human life. Intentional or not, the powers that be have determined that you are now sentenced to serve as a Grim Reaper until the day you crumble to dust and cease to exist altogether. Your trainer is waiting for you. Follow me."

Without waiting for a response, she turns swiftly on her sandaled foot and heads down the hall in long, confident strides.

My mind shifts through a range of emotions I might have once felt. Anger, terror, shock. But they are swallowed by the void as soon as the concept manifests, and I do nothing but obediently follow.

The hallway is long, windowless, and lined with evenly spaced identical doors. It's as bleak as any office I've ever seen, and I suddenly realize I can no longer visualize any other office. Surely, I had been in at least one before. The concept is familiar to me, and this skeletal being just said I was once human – another concept I know and understand. But there are no connections to these words. Not anymore.

A fluttering of panic bypasses whatever mental block has been placed inside my skull, and it alights in my chest for the briefest of moments before being consumed by the hollowness.

My guide stops in front of a door no different from any of the others and pushes it open. Inside, a Reaper identical to the one I've been following is waiting. Save for a missing front tooth and the number *1991* stitched onto their robe, there's no way I'd be able to tell them apart.

Reaper #986 gives me a curt nod, scribbles something on her clipboard, then gestures to #1991. "Reaper #2311, this will be your trainer, Reaper #1991. He is extremely skilled in the art of death and has molded many new recruits into pristine and exceptional Reapers. I have every confidence that he will do the same for you."

Reaper #1991's skull tilts just slightly, and I get the distinct feeling he's sizing me up. I catch myself trying to hold my breath and realize I no longer have lungs.

"Welcome to HQ, kid," he says, his voice gruff. "Hope you're a quick learner."

"I am." Something about the phrase feels right. I think I was given that compliment in the past.

"Good." He claps a hand on my shoulder bone and directs me to the door. "Let's rock and roll."

"You will receive your desk assignment, locker, and scythe once you've completed training," Reaper #986 says as I'm guided into the hallway once more. "Welcome to the team, dear."

"Um, thank you," I mutter, but I doubt she heard.

Reaper #1991 wastes no time with pleasantries. He points out a breakroom crowded with other black-cloaked Reapers as we pass, then leads me into a locker room stretching endlessly with thousands of gray, rusting lockers. The sounds of slamming doors and distant chatter can be heard as we make our way through the labyrinth.

"This one here's mine," #1991 says as he finally comes to a stop in front of a locker labeled with the same number stitched on his robe. He gives the built-in combination lock a few spins then tugs the door open, revealing nothing but a long-handled scythe resting inside. He takes it and holds it out to me, so I think he expects me to admire the tool. Gently, I tap the blade with my bony finger, and he continues, "Just sharpened her yesterday, so she's ready to go."

Sliding a hand into his robe's pocket, he retrieves a single white envelope.

"They're only going to give me one assignment at a time for today, so you can get the hang of how things work around here. But basically, you'll get assignments on your desk every morning, and you've got to complete them within that day."

"How many assignments can I expect to get?" I ask only because I feel like I should. Somehow, the answer doesn't surprise me.

"Anywhere from a couple to a couple dozen depending on the day. Things are pretty peaceful for the humans right now, so it's not like we get to team up on battlefields and cut wicks like weeds." He lets out a forlorn sigh that whistles through the gap from his missing tooth. "Those were the days."

"Wicks," I echo, and the image of a human candle comes to mind.

"You'll see." He rests the scythe in the crook of his arm and tears open the envelope, nodding along to the words written inside. "Tamara Lane. Sarasota, Florida. Probably some retiree, dammit."

"And that's a bad thing?" He's already stuffing the paper back into his pocket and then he takes off. I scurry along close behind.

"Not bad, just boring," he says. "The Assigned Deaths usually are. Old people, sick people, sometimes an accident. It's all predictable. The Random Deaths are where you can really let loose and get creative."

I don't say anything, and he takes it as a cue to continue.

"See, every month we Reapers are given a quota to fill. Thirty Random Deaths. That means we can pick anyone, anywhere, at any time in their life and off them. I'll show you after we take care of this old hag. I still got a couple more Random Deaths to reach my quota for this month."

I remain quiet as we fall into a line of Reapers waiting for something and mull over this new information. Dozens of assignments a day on top of thirty just-for-the-hell-of-it kills. That's a whole lot of death. Then again, that's who I am now. Better get used to it.

#1991 gestures ahead of us. "Up there's the Transportation Room. There's almost always a line. Death never sleeps, you know." He chuckles as if he's told some hilarious joke.

"You never feel tired? Not even after a long day of killing?"

This time, his laugh is loud and hearty, and a few other Reapers surrounding us join in.

"Newbie," he explains, which is met with a few nods and murmurings of understanding. His hand clamps down onto my shoulder. "Don't worry, kid. Before long, you won't even remember what being tired feels like."

I'm not sure I like the sound of that, but I nod and try to smile before realizing I can no longer do that. I settle for parting my jaw just a bit to simulate the expression.

The Transportation Room is made from ancient limestone lining the walls and ceiling and dripping with condensation. Etched into the packed dirt floor are rows upon rows of chalk circles surrounded with ancient symbols. I watch as the Reaper ahead of us steps into one and disappears in a flash of bright blue light.

#1991 grips my arm and pulls me into an open circle. "Stay close," he instructs. "Wouldn't want to leave you behind."

I stare at the symbols dancing around my feet. "How does this work?"

"Ancient magic," he says as if that explains everything. "You just think where you want to go, and you'll be taken there. If you ever feel like getting a surprise, you can just think *anywhere,* and you'll be dropped someplace random. Kind of like roulette. But for now, we're going to Florida."

The blue light envelops us before I can get another word in. Instinctively, I want to close my eyes against the harsh brightness, but then I remember I no longer have eyelids and settle for covering my eye sockets with my hands. Even then, the blue light seeps through the gaps in my bones.

When the light fades, we are standing in a bedroom designed to look like home. However, the red emergency button by the twin bed and the quiet, muffled voices speaking in the hallway beyond the door give away the setting for what it really is: a place where people go to die. And I guess we're here to help them along.

A figure is in the bed, pulling in the slow, even breaths of deep sleep. Coarse black hair fans out on the crisp white pillow beneath her head, and the deep lines engraved near the old woman's mouth reveal a lifetime of laughter.

"See that?" #1991 gestures to the woman's head, where a stub of a wick glows softly against the dark contrast of her hair. Like a candle with a flame that's about to peter out, the wick flickers. "Means it's time for her to go." He readies his scythe and steps up to her bedside.

"What happens if you just let her be?" I ask, my feet glued to my spot in the corner of the room.

"She couldn't die," #1991 says as if it's all so simple. "She'd just lay here, lifeless but not dead, and everyone would wonder why she can't just let go. I've seen it happen before when I can't get to an assignment fast enough. Now come here."

He flicks his wrist, impatience growing, and I step forward. As I approach the bedside of Tamara Lane, I'm struck with an onslaught of memories that don't belong to me. Children, a husband, grandchildren. Laughter. So much laughter, warm and rich. It echoes within my skull as if the woman were laughing along to some hilarious story. I see her. Not as she is now, old and dying, but as she was. Young and vibrant, carrying a babbling baby on her hip. Talking with friends. And then sobbing. So much sobbing. Someone has died. As I step closer, I see it is her husband. My heart aches for this woman and the immense sadness she must endure, and then I remember I no longer have a heart, but the feeling doesn't fade. The void isn't coming to my rescue this time.

What's happening to me? These visions, as clear and vivid as if these memories are playing out in the here and now, will not leave me. I see everything. Life. Death. Joy. Sorrow. Anger. From childhood to this very moment, the life of Tamara Lane plays out before me, and I can't take it anymore.

My jaw falls open, a silent scream escaping from my lungless chest as I fall to my knees and clap my hands against my skull, though the gesture does nothing to block it all out.

As I cower in child's pose, I hear the shuffling of sandaled feet and know #1991 has moved to stand beside me. Slowly, I raise my head and force the visions into the background as I try to focus on the permanently grinning skull looking down on me.

"You get used to it," he says.

"What is this?" I whisper. My bones are trembling, but I have no muscles to tighten so I can make it stop.

#1991 only shrugs and holds out a hand to help me back on my feet. "We get a glimpse of their life when we approach with an intent to kill. Don't know why. It's always been that way."

I stumble to my feet and brush invisible dirt from my robe. "That was more than a glimpse!"

#1991 shrugs again. "Don't know what to tell you. I don't make the rules."

"Who does?"

"The Big Boss, I guess."

"You guess?!"

He sighs heavily, the rush of forced air whistling through his missing tooth. "Look, this is just the way it is. Doesn't matter why we can see it. All that matters is completing our assignment. The faster you learn to tune it out, the better."

"How can you just tune something like that out?" My knees clack together as I look over at the woman sleeping peacefully, with no idea that Death is looming right beside her. Multiple Deaths. Arguing, at that. "Her life has been so full."

"And it's over now." #1991 turns away from me, effectively ending the conversation, and raises his scythe above Tamara's head. "Look, you want to get the blade at the very base of the wick, just so. All it takes is one pull, and...done."

The scythe makes a clean cut, and the glow fades into nothing-ness. The woman's chest stills, and her facial features take on a waxy appearance. I reach out to take her hand, as if on instinct, as if I could somehow comfort her in this moment of finality. But #1991 turns on his heel and heads for the window before I can touch her.

"Let's go. I'll show you how to really have fun."

I'm convinced that we have differing ideas of fun, but I don't know what else I can possibly do, so I follow my trainer like a good little trainee.

We stay in the area, walking on the sidewalk amongst the humans like we belong there. A young woman passes right through my skeletal frame, and she shivers as I instinctively apologize for running into her. Reaper #1991 finds this hilarious.

"You get used to being invisible, too," he assures me as he stifles his laughter. "But it is interesting when the human gets a little chill from us."

"I suppose." I swivel my head, taking in the sea of bobbing wicks that surround me. Some trail so high up, I can't see where they taper off against the backdrop of the cloudy sky. Others are so short; I wonder if their owner is suffering from some invisible disease. It strikes me that I could find out if I only decide to approach them. But something deep within me warns me away from doing that. I don't want to know.

#1991 stops suddenly, and I nearly collide into his back. His empty eye sockets appear to be fixated on a little girl skipping happily ahead of her caretaker and humming a merry tune. Then, his head tilts and his focus is now on the street, where several cars blatantly ignore the speed limit as they roar by.

"No," I whisper, but #1991 is already heading for the girl in long, determined strides.

"Keep up!" he calls over his shoulder.

I hurry to catch up and dart my gaze around in an attempt to find someone, anyone, to distract him from the plan he's so obviously hatching.

"We can't do too much to manipulate the world around us," he explains as he raises his free hand into the air, "and we definitely can't mess with any kind of free will, but we can jostle some stuff around. You just have to think about what you want to happen. Like this." He flicks his fingers, and I can only watch in dumbstruck horror as the scene plays out before me.

A potted plant falls from a balcony above the sidewalk, right next to the little girl, who jumps out of the way with a catlike reflex, off the sidewalk and onto the street. Right in front of a speeding car.

The adult keeping watch over her doesn't even scream until after the impact, it all happens so quickly. The child's mangled and bloodied body is thrown to the side. Tires squeal. The driver appears to register what they've done, and their foot hits the gas. They escape the scene, leaving nothing but a trail of burnt rubbery skid marks and bright red blood in their wake.

I refuse to approach as a crowd gathers around the little girl, who is wheezing through a mouthful of blood. Sirens are already wailing in the distance, but #1991 makes quick work of his kill. Her long, beautiful wick is severed from her body, and someone in the cluster of onlookers cries out, "I think she's dead!"

Reaper #1991 saunters over to me carrying an air of accomplishment, and I suspect if he could, he would be beaming with pride. "That's a good Random. Something about those screams really keeps me going."

I'm horrified, but I force my jaw to remain closed to keep from saying so. Right here and now, I vow to never take a child unless assigned to do so. At least then, they'd need the gentle release of death. If I have to be a Reaper, then that is the kind of Reaper I will become.

A flash of blue lightning strikes overhead, and a single piece of paper flutters down. A plain ballpoint pen is clipped to the side. #1991 reaches up and takes it without even looking.

"So, this is the Random Death Report Sheet," he explains as he unfolds the paper against the exterior wall of a quiet restaurant. "We're required to fill these out after each Random Death."

"Why?" I skim over the three simple, but grotesque questions printed neatly on the paper.

Name of Executed.

Reason for Execution.

Method of Execution.

"For the clerical Reapers," he explains as he begins carefully filling out the sheet. "They need a record on file, so they know we're keeping up with our quotas."

"But why the questions?" I follow his pen strokes as he makes them and realize he has the choppy handwriting of a serial killer. This should not be a surprise. He very likely was one.

Maddingly, he shrugs away my question again. "Like I said, they need a record on file."

Name of Executed: Carla Holden

Reason for Execution: Felt like it.

Method of Execution: Hit and run.

Something, somewhere, deep inside of me feels sick.

He caps the pen and tosses it up in the air along with the completed worksheet of death, and both disappear in another electric blue flash.

Brushing his hands together with an unnerving clicking sound, he turns to me and offers a curt nod. "Let's go see if I've got another assignment. I'll let you give the next one a try."

"Lucky me," I say, and he finds my sarcasm amusing.

"You'll get the hang of it. Really. Just takes some getting used to."

"I'm sure I will," I say as he taps his scythe on the ground three times, and a blinding light surrounds us. But I highly doubt that will ever happen.

REAPER #1632

Instead of an envelope on my desk, I find a single red sheet of paper printed with GUARD DUTY - INNER in bold, ornate script. Ever since my run-in with Steven Kelton, I've been receiving this assignment more and more frequently. The Big Boss must be nervous about me accidentally revealing the big secret. Or he's keeping an eye on me, watching for the same changes Steve suffered through. Maybe both.

Regardless, I can't abandon my post, as unnecessary as it may be. The Big Boss needs guards like a Grim Reaper needs life insurance.

With dragging feet, I make my way to the office and show my assignment to the guards outside the door. Wordlessly, they force open the heavy wood and I step into the marble-lined cavern. My partner for the day is already there, standing obediently against the wall, spine straight with attention. The numbers stitched onto his robe freeze me in place.

"Good morning, Reaper #1632," the Big Boss greets with a bright glow in his eye sockets. "This is Reaper #2007."

With a neck as stiff as rigor mortis, I offer the newbie a nod in greeting. For the moment, it's all I can do.

"#2007 has just completed his Reaper training," the Big Boss continues, "and today he will learn guard duty. I trust you will explain the intricacies to him."

There's not much to explain, but I bob my skull anyway and force the tightness to dissipate. "Yes, sir."

"It's nice to meet you." #2007 holds out his hand to me, an after-effect from his human life. Soon, these instincts will fade away. Grim Reapers have no need for pleasantries.

But I complete the gesture regardless, and our fingerbones click together as our hands shake. "The pleasure is mine," I say, and I mean it. Five years of waiting for this moment, and I can't seem to process that it's actually here. I will have to report this exciting news to my friend. It's been quite a while since we've last spoken. We can't risk raising suspicion.

Slowly, but surely, our plan is coming together.

Now, to begin the next step. I must befriend #2007.

Friendships are uncommon amongst the Reapers. What we have is more of a sick comradery, bonding over kills and sharing creative tips. But I will make an exception for #2007. Everything Steven Kelton lived, died, and lived again for depends on what happens next.

Flanking either side of the door, facing the Big Boss as he sits upon his velvet throne and waits for something to happen, I keep my watch while mentally compiling a slew of questions I once referred to as "small talk."

STEVE

I survey the boxes placed haphazardly throughout the living room, admiring the way they fill the conversation pit that's quickly going out of style. A shame, really, that this house built with modern touches in mind is already past its prime. I don't mind, though. It's the reason I was able to buy it for a steal.

I still chuckle at the reactions from everyone at Kelton Financial Services (formally Kelton and Gray Financial Services) when I announced my departure. Fortunately, some seemed to be prepared for the blow. After all, their bigwig CEO suffered a betrayal, a loss, and survived a suicide attempt all in a matter of months. Anyone would snap under that kind of pressure. And for a while, I suppose I did. Now, though, I'm saner than I ever was.

And that's really saying something.

The torch has been passed to Bob, who has exceeded my expectations in regard to his competency while I was going through the wringer. I'm almost proud of the big lug. Now, I exist as a silent CEO of sorts, raking in paychecks while those below me handle the real work. The American dream.

In my brief encounters with Heather, I managed to glean some important facts, like where she grew up. Thankfully she wasn't an army brat or anything that would have required her to be moved around a lot as a kid. I know where she was born, and I know she stayed in town until she went away to college. So, for the next phase of the Big Plan, I settle myself in the rapidly growing city of O'Fallon, Illinois, just outside of St. Louis. Now that I'm here, I have nothing left to do but wait, which is probably why I haven't fully unpacked despite coming up on my third anniversary in this house.

My life has taken on a very predictable routine. A morning walk, a class at the community center, an occasional phone call from my sister, Louise, and staring at the box containing my typewriter before drowning out the monotony with television until I eventually fall asleep in my easy chair with a few crumpled cans of beer at my feet.

What a life.

As I so often find myself doing, I'm standing at the base of the conversation pit and contemplating finally unpacking those boxes when a flash brightens the room from the corner of my eye. Tilting my head, I find my old, black-cloaked friend standing beside the bare bookshelf.

"Haven't seen you since the hospital," I remark as I turn to face #1632. "I assume this means you have news?"

"He's arrived."

The message would sound cryptic if I didn't know exactly what he was talking about. Even though I knew it would happen sooner or later, the relief that floods my body is palpable, and I slump to the floor so I can fully absorb the announcement. "And? How's he doing?"

"He's taken well to life at HQ." #1632 shifts from foot to foot for a moment. "Perhaps the sense of humanity you spoke of will come later."

"Probably." My fingers curl into the shag carpeting as I think over our plan. We still have fifteen long years to go. "Maybe he needs a nudge."

#1632 vehemently swivels his skull at the suggestion. "I refuse to interfere with that process. He could report me for feeling any sort of humanity and I could lose my skull before our plan comes to fruition. The rules are still too fresh in his mind."

I frown, realizing impatience is already getting the better of me. This is the long-haul stage of the Big Plan and, damn it, I am in it to win it. "Right. That wouldn't be smart."

"My current goal is to grow close with #2007 without raising any suspicion," #1632 announces, and I snort back a jolt of sarcastic laughter. I can't help it.

"Careful, you might stir up rumors of an office romance. Now *that* would create some juicy gossip around the Elixir pot."

"Grim Reapers are not capable of romantic feelings," #1632 says as if I didn't already know. What a buzzkill. "But I am being cautious in my approach. Currently, I am engaging #2007 with small talk in the break room. He seems happy to chat."

"That's a start," I say with a nod of approval.

His head tilts to the side and I realize he's looking at my shoulder. "How's the arm?"

Raising it above my head as high as it can go, I rotate my shoulder to show off my almost full range of motion. "It'll always be a little stiff, but it was worth it for the cause."

He nods, then swivels his skull around the living room. "It seems your life has changed in many ways since your so-called death."

"The Big Boss still thinks you offed me?"

"Yes." His arms cross, and he leans back against the wall as if we're having a casual chat about how rainy the weather has been lately. "He's been keeping a much closer eye on me lately, though. I am assigned inner guard duty more often than not these days. But I believe he's doing it out of concern that I may reveal the secrets of your misadventures. I don't think you have anything to worry about."

The sigh of relief that escapes my lungs relaxes my entire body. I didn't realize how much stress I'd been carrying in the absence of my friend. If our plan is discovered, he would surely lose his skull. And I'm sure some elaborate scheme to end my life for good would likely be orchestrated by the Big Boss.

"Do me a favor and try to visit a little more often, would you?" With a shudder, I get back on my feet. "When you don't show up for five years, part of me wonders if you've been executed. And it's not like Reaper Headquarters has a business number I can call to check in on you."

He chuckles, but his words are sincere. "I apologize for worrying you. Perhaps we should schedule check-ins in advance. If I don't arrive on time, then you would know you'd have reason to worry."

I nod and head to the kitchen to retrieve the pinup calendar nailed to the wall. Miss April stares up at me with her pouty red lips and cleavage on full display. The look in her deep brown eyes reminds me of Susan, and for a moment, I have to close my eyes. When I'm ready, I pry them open again and flip through the months. "How about a quarterly review? The third Tuesday. That would put our next meeting on July 21st. Does that work for you?"

"I believe I can pencil you in," he says, and the sarcastic undertone makes me smile. I've forgotten what it's like to have a normal conversation with someone I consider a friend. I haven't allowed myself to get close to anyone in my community center classes, especially the more elderly members, and I haven't conversed beyond the standard greetings and pleasantries in nearly five years now. The realization produces a sinking in my chest.

"You probably shouldn't stay too long," I say, attempting to mask my reluctance.

"Yes," he agrees with a nod. "I'll see you in July, then."

I gesture around at the unpacked boxes. "I'll be here."

For a moment, he seems to take in the weight of my newly adapted minimalist, hermit lifestyle. I didn't do it on purpose, but the less hazards I have to face on a daily basis, the better. I can't risk anything. I rarely even drive anymore.

"Be well, Steven Kelton," he says. And in a blue flash, he's gone.

REAPER #2311

I've adapted well to life here. It was surprisingly easy to become a killer, slicing wicks day and night. I suppose easing into the job so quickly shouldn't come as a shock. After all, killing is how I got here. How many and how often, though, I can't imagine. Many Reapers here insist the deaths they caused as a human were accidental. I wonder if the life or lives I ended were unintentional as well. In the end, though, there's no real way any of us could know. I suppose we all just need a way to feel better.

My training is now finished. The Big Boss commended me for how swiftly the process was completed. I may even be on track to receive the coveted Reaper of the Month placard if I keep up my hard work.

My assignments for today are simple. Six envelopes are on my desk this morning, all featuring the elderly. On days like these, the world feels a little more at peace. An odd twinge pulls somewhere deep inside me when a child's name is written on my assignment sheet.

Time passes. How much, I couldn't even guess.

With my elderly appointments taken care of, I head to the break room with plans to execute a few Random Deaths to close out the workday. The tables are bustling with Reapers cradling white mugs filled with a swirling purple liquid, chatting and sharing tales of their kills. With no esophagus or internal organs, we can't actually drink the Elixir. It's simply a prop, one designed to create a sense of normalcy around here, or so I assume. There's something just so human about holding a mug of hot liquid and shooting the breeze with a coworker. I find myself looking forward to the daily ritual. I do wish I could taste the Elixir though. I can't fathom a guess as to what it tastes like, since I have no olfactory senses to even know what it smells like.

Mug in hand, I make my way to a table in a corner, where a Reaper with a shiny steel plate bolted over his right temple sits. #4821 and I aren't exactly friends. Those simply don't exist here. But we have become friendly with each other, as we began our training around the same time, and, as in all workplaces, newbies must stick together. He raises his mug to me as I pull out the chair opposite him and sit.

"Busy day?" he asks. He raises the mug and stops when the ceramic rim knocks against his teeth. We all forget sometimes.

"Nothing major." I dip my fingerbone into the glimmering liquid and swirl it. I feel like I have to do something with it. "Only old folks today. It was their time, all they needed was an escort."

#4821 nods, and he remains quiet for a moment. "Do you ever feel like we don't belong here, #2311?"

My jaw tightens, the rest of my skeletal frame following suit. I know dangerous words when I hear them. I must tread carefully. "No."

He senses the lie. I don't need his facial expression to tell me that. He lowers his voice, well aware of the danger he's putting himself in. "I want to know what I did to land myself here."

"You killed someone," I remind him through clenched teeth. "We all did."

"I know *that*. But don't you want to know the details?"

"I don't need to." But I have often wondered. I look down at my black-cloaked lap. "We shouldn't be talking about this."

"I just can't help it," he laments, more to himself than to me. "We deserve to know. For all we're forced to do here, we deserve to know exactly what we did to get to this place."

I waver slightly because I don't disagree. "What difference would it make?"

He lets out a long sigh and reaches up to scratch at the edge of the metal plate as if it itched. Another force of habit, I suppose. "I guess you're right."

"There's no point in dwelling on it," I whisper, leaning in close to ensure he hears me but no one else around does. So far, everyone seems too absorbed in their own conversations. "Just drop it. You know what will happen if you don't."

"Have you ever considered that execution might be better than this?" The hollowness in his voice sends a shiver down my spine, and I stand abruptly.

"I have to work on my quota."

He looks up at me, and the sadness radiating from him does nothing to ease the sense of apprehension settling into my bones. "Find some good ones."

"I always do."

With that, I dump the contents of my mug into the sink and set it in the bin to be washed. As I head for the Transportation Room, I consider who to take as a Random today. An older person, most likely. Maybe middle aged. Perhaps I can find someone with a sickness eating away at their insides.

But only adults. No children.

Never children.

REAPER #1632

Time passes differently for Reapers. Every day is filled with the monotony of sameness, the hours spent at Headquarters punctuated between brutal and calculated deaths. We are a necessary evil, and the days slip by unnoticed save for the dates printed on our assignment sheets. With no need for sleep, seconds tick by with nothing to separate us from the endless days stretching ahead. Years slip into obscurity with nothing to show for them and no core memories to look back on.

My centennial anniversary has come and gone. As expected, I was celebrated with the gift of a large solo assignment, carried out with a small audience to marvel at my hard work and dedication. Twenty men in war-torn trenches, eaten alive by a deadly bacterium that spread so quickly they were dead within hours thanks to my swiftness. The applause from my adoring colleagues was thunderous. The light fading from their bloody eyes still haunts me in the quiet moments, which are frequent now due to my constant guard duty assignments.

I've lost count of the days since my last Assigned Death, and while I am given enough time to ensure my monthly quotas are met, inner guard duty has become my life. Steve is aware of the chokehold the Big Boss has on me these days, but I visit as frequently as I can. Oftentimes, I feel the Big Boss's smoldering eye sockets boring into me as I stand straight against the wall. Sometimes, I wonder if he knows, and he is simply biding his time until he is able to remove my skull from my spine.

Nothing of interest happens, and I lose track of time as day slips into night and back again. #2007 often flanks me on guard duty, and I can't help but notice he's grown quieter lately. I am coming up with a tactical way to probe him when a gong reverberates overhead, signaling a shift change.

Wordlessly, #2007 turns to open the heavy doors for our replacements waiting patiently on the other side. He walks off, and I take a step forward to follow him into the breakroom when the Big Boss raises a massive, bony hand to stop me.

"#1632," he bellows. "Stay a moment, would you?"

Nothing about this can be good.

With reluctance, I head for the throne. If I had a heart, it'd be sinking into my chest as the Big Boss instructs the new inner guards to wait outside.

No, this is certainly not good.

The heavy wooden door is pulled closed, the ancient carvings illuminated by the flickering eternal flames inside their deep ebony sconces. The light reflects on my bones as well as I walk the long path to the throne, the Big Boss's visage growing larger and larger the closer I get.

He waits until I come to a stop in front of him. For a moment, I wonder if I should get down on one knee and offer a swift bow. It seems appropriate for someone who holds my fate in their bony hands. The ancient scythe's blade shimmers as if I needed a reminder of that. But before I can bend down, the Big Boss speaks.

"It's been many years since the...*incident,*" he remarks.

I consider my options for a response and decide less is more. "Indeed."

The Big Boss stares me down with those flickering red eye sockets, and if I still had skin, my robe would be drenched in sweat. What is he getting at?

"I suppose you've noticed I've been keeping a close eye on you."

Some instinctive part of me tries to pull a gulp of air into lungs that no longer exist. It's been over a year since I last saw Steven Kelton, toiling away in his little home until the time to act comes. Surely the Big Boss has not been biding his time for a punishment. He is a Reaper of prompt action. If he knew of my visits to the man who is supposed to be long dead, I would have been executed by now. So, what could he possibly be getting at with this little private chat?

"Considering the unprecedented events that unfolded, you understand why I could not simply allow you to resume duties as normal," he continues, and I nod. "But you have proven that I am able to trust you after all, Reaper #1632. You have diligently remained at your post when requested while still finding time to complete assignments and your monthly quota. You are a commendable employee, and I was right to allow you to live, for lack of a better term."

"Just another cog in the machine," I mutter as quietly as I can, the words escaping with no command from me.

The Big Boss's hand arcs around the spot where an ear once was. "Come again?"

I straighten my shoulders and raise my skull. "I said, thank you, sir."

He nods, satisfied. "It is with great pride that I award you with the Reaper of the Month plaque. You'll find it on your desk when you return."

"I'm honored," I say, though my tone suggests I am anything but.

"I presume you are tired of such constant guard duty." The Big Boss flicks his wrist as he speaks and gives a quick shake of his head. "I am concerned that the others might grow suspicious if I continue assigning you so much."

My interest piques at this. Is the freedom I once enjoyed here at Headquarters going to be bestowed upon me again? It was only an illusion, of course, but it was better than nothing. And it would allow me to visit my friend more frequently. I assume he is growing more and more anxious as the time approaches to execute our plan, and I'd like to be there to offer some semblance of reassurance. I remain silent and wait for the Big Boss to continue.

"I can't just let you go from such frequent guard duty right away, however," he continues, and my shoulders slump within my robe. "But I will be easing you off. Is that an agreeable arrangement for you, Reaper #1632? You will be granted more, shall we say, *enticing* assignments in exchange."

Those flickering embers are fixated on me, searching for a reaction, or perhaps a cheer of excitement for such an offer. I give him what he's looking for and bob my skull enthusiastically, my spine popping with the movement. "Yes, sir. Thank you."

I shudder to think of what the Big Boss considers "enticing."

I am dismissed with another flick of the wrist, and the two new guards waiting outside the door eye me with mild curiosity as I push open the doors and breeze past. With a sense of relief and a less watchful eye on me, I head straight for the breakroom to hunt down #2007. I have put this off for much too long, and the time is approaching fast.

STEVE

The time is getting closer, and I feel dreadfully unprepared. As I turn my wall calendar over from 1998 to 1999, a fluttering of anxiety alights in my chest, and my heart gives a little squeeze. The feeling isn't too uncommon these days. Sometimes I wonder if I'm just getting old and I'm on the verge of a heart attack. That kind of twisted bullshit would happen to me right when we're nearing the end of it all. But I know it's just my body itching to do something other than wait.

Needing some sort of action, I wander into the living room and settle into my beloved conversation pit with my bulky laptop balanced on my knees. The sporadic short stories that have been published in literary magazines here and there over the years have kept me working at least a little bit. When you become a recluse, you need something to occupy your time.

But I barely have the word "*The*" typed out when a blue crackle flashes in the corner of my eye. With a sense of pleasant surprise, I twist my neck to find #1632 standing by my bookshelf, now stuffed with dogeared tomes.

"Long time no see," I remark as I push my laptop closed. Its hinges squeak in protest.

"There's been progress," #1632 says. Always straight to the point with this guy.

Leaning forward, I set my laptop on the coffee table and stand. "Want to tell me about it over some coffee? It's from this morning, but I think it's still warm enough." I laugh at my own joke but head into the kitchen anyway. Just because he can't have any doesn't mean I can't either.

#1632 trails behind me, his skull swiveling as he looks around my humble abode. "You've unpacked."

"I needed to do something." I grab a clean mug from the dishwasher and fill it with the last few ounces of coffee from the pot. It's cold and tastes like crap, but I remember what it's like to not have tastebuds and savor it anyway. "Now tell me what's going on."

He nods and leans against the counter, crossing his bony arms over his chest. The gesture is so casual, I almost have to laugh. "First of all, the Big Boss will not be keeping such a close eye on me anymore."

"So, that's why you're here."

He offers a curt nod and continues. "You must think I've been slacking off, but I'm sure you recall how so-called friendship works at Headquarters. Anything outside of bragging over assignments is considered odd."

"How could I forget?" I shudder at the memories of my horrible attempts to strike up conversations back in my time as a Reaper. No wonder the Big Boss was suspicious.

"But #2007 has been slowly warming up to me," #1632 says. "And it's happening."

"What is?"

"The sparks."

"Ah." I nod and sip at the icy coffee. "His humanity is starting to come back. Finally. I was getting worried."

"Why would you worry?" #1632 tilts his skull to the side. "You knew it would happen. He told you himself."

"Yes, but that was a different timeline."

#1632 is silent for a moment. "I'm not sure I understand all this alternate timeline nonsense."

"Neither do I, but I try not to dwell on it too much." I chuckle. "This is good, though. The assignment to take Heather's father in that car crash is only a few months away now. #2007 needs to be made aware of what's about to happen. Do you think he's ready?"

He appears to think it over for a second, then his skull tilts forward and back in a slow nod. "Today, after the Big Boss asked to speak to me in private, I tracked down #2007 in the breakroom."

"And?"

A slow intake of air is sucked in between #1632's teeth, and it makes a high-pitched whistling sound. "And he was concerned that I was also being reprimanded for having...human feelings."

"Oh shit." I let out a long breath through pursed lips and shake my head. "It's already happening then. And you haven't noticed?"

1632's skull dips down in an apologetic bow. "You must think I've failed you."

I shake my head. "If his sense of humanity was obvious enough for you to notice, he'd be dead. Or whatever it is that happens to executed Reapers. It's a good thing the Big Boss noticed first, trust me."

"You have given me no reason to doubt you yet, Steven Kelton." #1632 crosses the room and eases into a chair pulled out from the kitchen table in a caricature of weariness. "I could not even get a word in before he began to ramble. He said we need to stick together; to hold each other accountable so we can both keep our skulls attached to our spines."

My mouth twists into a frown. "He did this in the break room?"

"No one overheard. Please, do not worry."

"And what did you say in response?" I run a hand through my hair and suck in the final sip of stale coffee. As if on impulse, I turn and begin setting up a fresh pot.

"Well, I couldn't very well tell him the real reason the Big Boss wished to speak with me."

Raising a brow, I pour coffee grounds into the filter. "You played along? I would have killed to see that." I pause. "Well, not literally, of course."

He ignores me and continues. "He knows he can trust me now."

"That's great." My eyes flick over to the calendar and that tight-ness squeezes at my chest again. "But we need to move faster than this."

"What do you propose we do?"

Pressing my lips into a thin line, I consider my words carefully.

What I'm about to suggest could easily end up getting at least two of us killed, maybe all three if the Big Boss is in a particularly foul mood, but this duo needs to become a trio and our time is running out.

"Tell #2007 everything. And once he knows, bring him to me."

REAPER #2311

Today is the day of Reaper #4821's execution. It will serve as a warning. Sympathizing with those we are assigned to kill is a crime of the highest caliber in Reaper Headquarters, and he will be an example to all of us.

I have no heart. Not anymore. But still, the horrific turn of events makes me sad. Now I have to watch the one Reaper I considered a friend lose his skull to the Big Boss's ancient, polished scythe, and I must remain stoic throughout unless I want to be next on the chopping block.

The courtroom within Headquarters is merely for show. If you're sentenced to appear in Reaper Court, the outcome has already been decided. Still, like playing out a scene in a movie, Reapers crowd into the stands to watch the execution unfold. It is a rare event around here, and most find the spectacle an enticing source of entertainment.

Chatter fills the courtroom as I squeeze my skeletal frame into a free space on a bench in the very back. The room is dim, lit only with flickering torches along the walls. The Big Boss sits at the judge's podium, a curled white wig sitting on top of his skull in a caricature of justice. He slams a gavel down, and the echo of wood-on-wood forces us all into silence.

We watch together as two guard Reapers escort #4821 into the center of the room. His skull hangs low, shoulders slumped, and he doesn't put up a fight as the guards drag his limp body to the stand where his spine will be severed. I wish I could send some encouraging thoughts his way, to let him know he has at least one friend in this room who will miss him. But I'm just another blank white skull in a sea of identical expressionless cogs.

The Big Boss rises from his seat and #4821 doesn't lift his skull to look at him. It's the ultimate disrespect, but it serves as a final middle finger to the oppressive system that has brought him here today.

"Grim Reaper #4821," the Big Boss booms, and the flames lining the walls flicker in a theatrical display of his authority, "you have been accused of sympathizing with the humans you are assigned to kill as well as slacking on your monthly quota. What do you have to say about this?"

#4821 is quiet for a long time. The sounds of creaking bones and rustling fabric fill the room as the other Reapers anxiously wait for a response. Finally, without moving his defeated body, he answers.

"I just can't do it anymore."

"You do not deny these accusations?" the Big Boss presses.

I guess he's trying to put on a show for everyone, trying to get some sort of reaction out of #4821 for the sake of entertainment. But #4821 refuses to give him the satisfaction, and the hollow space between my ribs swells with a sense of pride. Quickly, I tamp it down lest anyone pick up on the fleeting emotion.

"No," is all #4821 says.

A few disappointed grumbles scatter amongst the crowd, and I lean forward on the bench to get a final look at my friend.

The Big Boss sighs then rises to his feet. "Very well. As you are well aware, your sentence is execution." He holds out his hands, and the ancient scythe, wrapped in ceremonial gold embossed cloth, is placed in his arms. He removes the cloth and steps up to the execution platform in long, meaningful strides. "Do you have any final words?"

The room goes quiet again. Someone in the crowd coughs, which is ridiculous since no one here has lungs. I guess that old, instinctual need to fill an awkward silence transcends even death.

Slowly, #4821 lifts his skull and meets the Big Boss's glowing eye sockets with a sense of disdain. "The show must go on, right?" In a flash, he swivels around, and I swear he's looking right at me. "Don't trust the system."

"Enough!" the Big Boss cries, and with a flick of his wrist, he commands the guards to grab #4821 by the arms and force him into a kneeling position. "You've had your say."

#4821's jaw tightens, and his teeth grit together. Suddenly, I'm struck with the urge to ask him about his final words. I need clarification. The system has been in place since the dawn of time. What part of it can't be trusted? Death is part of the natural circle of life, and Reapers are required to keep that cycle going. Is there something going on here, behind the scenes, that no one thinks to question?

Terrifyingly, I find myself rising to my feet, the words ready to spring free from between my teeth, and I catch myself before I can guarantee my own execution. Luck is on my side, and the other Reapers are beginning to stand as well so they can get the best view of #4821's demise.

I clutch at my black robe, keeping my arms locked firmly at my sides as the blade comes down. It whistles as it slices through the dense air. #4821 doesn't flinch when the scythe meets his spine, and I find myself wishing for eyelids, so I don't have to watch. But looking away will raise suspicion, so I try to force my vision to lose focus for the final cut.

His spine severs with a snapping sound, like a rubber band flinging across a room. #4821's skull drops to the floor with a hollow thud. It bounces once, twice, then rolls off the platform and comes to a stop at the Big Boss's feet. I thought a Reaper's eye sockets were devoid of life before, but there is something truly dead about the blackness within #4821's now. They stare up at the Big Boss, as if accusatory, and then, with a scoff, the Big Boss kicks the nuisance out of his way.

I let out a sharp gasp – I can't help it – and a sense of panic immediately floods my head with a thudding sensation. But no one heard. The applause and whistles and cheers are too loud, and they drown out my indignation with their celebration.

As they cheer on the final death of their colleague, I wonder why it's such a crime to feel saddened by the taking of lives. Of course, many of the Reapers here are incapable of feeling such an emotion. I don't know if they were like that as a human as well, or if it's some kind of coping mechanism needed to keep up with this horrific life. I guess killing day in and day out does require a special kind of Reaper to not completely lose your mind. But I know I will never be one of those Reapers. Try as I might, I just can't shake these bursts of emotion that course through my body. And I don't want to, either.

A shudder races up my spine with electric fingers as I realize I'll be next on the execution stand if anyone were to discover this. As I file out of the courtroom amongst the disappointed mutterings of my coworkers, I resolve to never let anyone see my true self. #4821 saw a crack of how I really feel inside, and even that was too risky. No more Elixir pot chats. No more mingling in the breakroom. I must distance myself from everyone at HQ if I want to keep my skull attached. As awful as this life is, the unknown which lies beyond the executioner's blade is far more terrifying. If I want out of here, I'll have to find a way to quit myself. On my terms.

I wonder if that's even possible.

On my desk, I find a slew of envelopes. Assignments have been pouring in for the Reapers who took some time off to witness the execution, and now I have to play catchup. I sift through their contents with a growing sense of dread. A few elderly, a sickly forty-something, and two children. Two. The assignments sicken me. But I have to complete them.

I decide to take care of the children first. Get those two over with. And I will not think about them as I do. I can't. Maybe there's an art to turning off your mind when you bring down your scythe.

I head for the Transportation Room in a sea of identical Reapers. I hear snippets of stories of kills they're most proud of. I overhear a few suggestions for spicing up the monotony of death. I want no part of it.

As I step into the chalk circle, surrounded by the bright, sparkling blue light, I wonder how much longer I can keep this up.

REAPER #1632

The breakroom is abuzz with ambient, indistinctive chatter, as it so often is. But I am not here for pleasantries or the illusion of sipping on a hot cup of joe. I find #2007 wedged into a corner, a white mug clasped in his skeletal fingers. His skull is tilted downward, his hood bunched at his shoulders, and the white bone gleams under the fluorescent lights.

As I approach, he straightens his shoulders, and he settles back against the wall with an air of relaxation. He truly believes we are allies in the same situation, and it is to my benefit that he continues to think this. I offer him a curt nod and make no effort to grab a mug of my own.

"#2007," I begin, keeping my voice low, "there is an urgent matter I must discuss with you."

He shifts and raises the mug halfway to his teeth before catching himself. "What is it?"

Although all the Reapers here appear to be caught up in their own conversations, I cannot take any chances. With a subtle shake of the head, I extend my pinky bone toward the exit. "Not here."

Taking the hint, #2007 is quick to dump out his Elixir. He heads for the door while I remain in place, scanning the blank, expressionless skulls for any signs of curiosity. I believe we are of no interest to anyone in the breakroom, but I count to one hundred before making my way to the exit myself.

#2007 is waiting for me just around the corner. His right leg shakes with anticipation, and I gesture for him to move further down the hall. There's no one here, but I keep several paces behind him just to be safe.

"What's wrong?" he whispers over his shoulder, but I only swivel my head again.

I realize I'm giving him the opportunity to overthink and assume the worst. Fortunately, I will soon be able to put his worries to rest.

Stopping in front of the file room, I catch his attention and motion for him to join me inside. He hesitates, then slips through the small crack I've created with the opened door. With one last look around the hallway, I duck inside the room and pull the door closed behind me with a soft click.

#2007 wrings his fingers together, and the anxious rattling of bones would be enough to give me a headache if I were still able to get them.

"What's this all about?" he asks, darting glances across the room. "Won't the clerical Reapers catch us in here?"

I reach out and place a hand on his shoulder in an attempt to be reassuring. "They do their filing every three hours on the dot, and they just finished their latest round. We have plenty of time."

He appears to relax, but only a little bit. With a whistling breath expelling through his teeth, he slumps against one of the tall, beige filing cabinets and meets my eye sockets. "Talk, #1632. Are you in trouble?" I don't how it's possible, but he almost seems to pale. "Has the Big Boss decided to make good on his execution threat?"

"No, no," I answer quickly. "What we need to discuss has nothing to do with the Big Boss and everything to do with Steven Kelton."

His skull cocks to the side. "Who is Steven Kelton?"

Slowly, my hand slides off his shoulder and drops back to my side. "It's complicated, but I assure you everything I am about to tell you is the absolute truth."

He shifts from foot to foot then adjusts the way his robe hangs on his skeletal frame. "Tell me what's going on. You're confusing me."

I chuckle. I can't help it. "My apologizes, but I'm afraid you'll be even more confused for a while."

"#1632," he says.

I acknowledge his impatience. No more stalling. I've pushed on this far, and there is no backing out now. I take in a long, unnecessary breath and begin to speak.

"Steven Kelton was once a Grim Reaper. Reaper #2497, to be exact. In another time."

"Another time—?"

I hold up a hand. "Please, just let me speak." He settles and I continue. "In this other time, you were acquainted with him. You connected with him much as you are connecting with me now. You warned him of the Big Boss's disdain for sympathy, as you saw the signs developing in #2497." His teeth part, and I can tell he wants to interrupt again, but I press on before he can get any words out. "Around that time, #2497, or Steve as he prefers, had come across a remarkable discovery – a human who could see Grim Reapers."

#2007 gasps. "That's not possible."

"I assure you, it is," I snap, growing impatient with his interruptions. "This human was called Heather, and in a few months, you will be assigned to cut her father's wick in a fatal car accident."

"How do you—?"

"Allow me to explain. Somehow, Steven Kelton was able to shift the timeline. I understand how confusing this sounds. Please, just listen. His desire for a second chance at humanity, and to escape the confines of the Reaper world, was so strong, he eventually asked this Heather woman to cut his wick with his own scythe. I don't know how, but this event sent him back to the year 1978, to the moment just before he made the decision to murder his coworker and condemn himself to the life of a Reaper. Only this time, he didn't do it.

"He couldn't remember anything about being a Reaper, but somehow he still changed his mind in that crucial instant. And then he realized he could see us, too."

I give #2007 a moment to let the information sink in. I realize I'm bombarding him with quite a lot. He doesn't speak this time, so I go on.

"For a while, he thought he was simply losing his mind. A natural, human reaction, I believe. But when I came across him on an assignment, and I realized he could see me, I had to investigate. But still, he didn't remember his time as a Reaper. Neither of us could come up with a plausible explanation for the onset of this ability. Until the Big Boss caught us and summoned us both to his office."

#2007 leans forward, fully invested now. "How are you still alive?"

"I have proven myself worthy of trust." My ribcage swells with a sense of undeserved pride, and a slump my shoulders in an effort to push it away. "But that's beside the point. When returning to the Reaper world, twenty years ago now, Steven Kelton's memories were unlocked. He remembered everything. The Big Boss took some time to decide how to handle such an unprecedented situation, and in the end, I was assigned to end Steve's life for the final time."

For a moment, #2007 is quiet. Then, he asks, "Why are you telling me all this?"

"Because Steven Kelton wants to save Heather from a life of witnessing the horrors of the Reapers, and he firmly believes the car accident you will be assigned to is the key."

"But—"

"Steven Kelton is alive," I announce, my voice low but firm. While #2007 absorbs the confession of my trickery against the Big Boss, I explain. "We devised a plan to make the Big Boss believe he was dead. I sliced only the tip of his wick. I wasn't sure if it would work, but it did. Ever since that day, Steve and I have been lying in wait for you to appear, and for the right time to tell you of our plan."

"What plan?" #2007 asks in a breathless whisper.

This time, I place both hands on his shoulders and squeeze. "We are going to prevent the car accident. Steve believes the near-death experience somehow unlocked Heather's ability to witness the Reapers. According to what you told Steve in the past – er, future, I suppose – you considered slicing Heather's wick as well, to save her from a life without her father. She is only a child now. Perhaps her young, susceptible age has something to do with it.

I'm not sure. But Steve is confident, and he has yet to steer me wrong."

#2007's hands go to the top of his skull, and he swivels his head back and forth. "This is crazy."

All I can do is nod in sympathy. "I understand. I have a difficult time fathoming the concept myself, but I assure you everything Steven Kelton has told me is true."

He takes in a few slow, deep breaths. Old habits die harder than humans. "So," he begins, "what is it you need me to do exactly?"

Good. This is progress.

I gesture to the door. "First, you must meet Steve. He will explain everything much better than I."

#2007 takes a step back. "Now?"

"He is expecting you."

His skull swivels around the dim, abandoned room. "How has the Big Boss not caught on?"

"As I said, he trusts me. And he has no reason to believe Steven Kelton isn't rotting in the Earth's soil as we speak."

The room falls quiet, and I give him some time to fully comprehend everything I've just told him. I hope he understands. I don't believe I was ever able to explain things properly. Hopefully, Steve can help clear up any lingering questions, although I think a bit of confusion will always remain.

"So," #2007 begins slowly, "for some inexplicable reason, one Reaper was able to reset their life and bypass the decision that got them here. They got to start over. How?"

"I do not know."

"How did the Big Boss react?"

I choke back a bark of sarcastic laughter. "Poorly. Such an event is unheard of."

"And why this man? Why Steve? I'm sure he wasn't the only Reaper who wanted to quit this corporate hell. I'm sure he wasn't the only one who wanted another shot at life. I'm sure many of us are bottling up those feelings right now." He looks down at his sandaled feet. "Myself included. And it can't possibly be a matter of just wanting it bad enough."

"Steven Kelton is an enigma, and I'm afraid that is the only reason he and I have been able to come up with."

#2007 arches his spine and puffs his ribcage out, creating the illusion of taking a deep breath. "Okay. I want to meet this man."

Pulling the door open, I extend my arm to the hall. "After you."

STEVE

A trill of excitement flutters up in my chest when my dinner preparations are interrupted by a bright blue flash. As usual, #1632 wastes no time with pleasantries.

"He's right behind me."

I set the knife I'd been using to chop onions down on the cutting board and wring my hands together in nervous anticipation. When #2007's form appears in the blank space beside #1632, I nearly spring forward to hug my old friend. But then I remember this version of #2007 has never met me, and a strange sense of disappointment deflates my eagerness.

Oddly enough, #2007 is the one to break the silence swelling in the room. "I would say I'm glad to see you again, but..."

"I explained everything as best I could," #1632 says, a hint of sheepishness in his voice.

Throwing my head back with a hearty laugh, I extend my hand to #2007. "I'll just say it's nice to see you after all these years."

He accepts the handshake with slight hesitation. "You really can see us."

I let go of his hand and throw my arms out wide. "Yes, indeed. I am the man, the myth, the legend. The big, dark secret the Big Boss fears. Reaper Headquarters' biggest mystery. The—"

"We understand, Steven Kelton," #1632 cuts me off, and I can't help but chuckle at his formal tone. Not for the first time, I wonder what year the human version of #1632 died and what he was like as a person. I suppose it's a mystery I'll never have an answer to.

I clear my throat. "Anyway, I'm willing to bet you have some questions for me." Pulling two chairs out from the table, I invite my otherworldly friends to sit. "Since you're actually here, I'm guessing that means you believe at least some of what #1632 here told you."

#2007 nods slowly as he lowers himself into the chair. He's delicate with his actions, like he's afraid it won't be able to hold his weight or something. "I guess it's just one of those stories that's so crazy and far-fetched, it has to be true."

"I get what you mean," I say with a wry smile. "So, let's cut to the chase. I take it #1632 filled you in on who I am and how I got here?"

"I believe he understands the situation," #1632 says, and #2007 bobs his skull in agreement. "Although he seems to be a bit befuddled by the timeline."

"Yeah, yeah, we all are." I dismiss the confusion with a wave of my hand. No use dwelling on something no human, or Reaper, I guess, was ever meant to understand. "All that matters is that we're here now, and we have a chance to undo what's going to happen to Heather. She lived in constant fear of seeing the Reapers, and considering she essentially saved my life, I'm going to return the favor."

#2007 spreads his hands on the tabletop, palms down. "And how, exactly, do you plan to do that."

Rising to my feet, I take strides back and forth across the room. This explanation requires pacing. "I've given that a lot of thought, and I think I've come up with the best plan." I nod at #2007. "First, I know the accident is going to happen in this town. That's why I moved here. But I don't know exactly where. So, as soon as you get the assignment, you come to me, and we'll go to the location together."

"But how will I—?"

"Her father's name is Victor Franklin," I say before he can finish. #2007 lets out a little huffing noise and settles back in his chair. I wonder what stick is up his bony butt. "Keep an eye out for that name."

"Right, I can do that," he says carefully, like he expects to be interrupted again. I glance at #1632, and he shrugs.

"Then," I continue, "we go to the intersection to wait. Plan A is that I'll try to prevent the accident, if possible. I don't know how yet because I don't know the details, but I've always been pretty good at coming up with plans on the fly. With no accident, his wick will shoot back up to a normal lifespan and your assignment will be cancelled."

"And when that inevitably fails?" #1632 asks dryly.

I squint at him. "Then we'll move on to Plan B. Although you may not like this one as much, #2007."

His skull is as hollow and blank as ever, but I can feel the suspicion seeping off of him. "What?"

"Just don't do it," I propose.

"Absolutely not!" #2007 cries as he shoots up to his feet. He slams his hands down on the table to really drive his point home. "I'm already in hot water with the Big Boss. If he thinks I might even be considering abandoning an assignment, I'll be executed on the spot!"

"Yeah, I figured you might feel that way," I say, motioning for him to sit back down. "That's why I came up with Plan C."

He plops back down in the chair and crosses his arms. "Why not get rid of Plan B altogether and make your Plan C the new Plan B?"

"Because I like to have all the options laid out," I say with a simple shrug. My right shoulder stiffens with the gesture. "Now, Plan C is probably our best bet. See, I think Heather gained the ability to see Reapers because you *almost* sliced her wick. You told me about it. You said you held your scythe there and contemplated for a long time. Actually, I suspect you may have actually put a little nick in her wick," I pause to chuckle at the rhyme, "and that's what unlocked the ability. That's all speculation, of course. I've had a lot of time to think about this."

#2007 throws his hands up in the air. "You should have led with that, Steve. That seems like the simplest plan. Let's just go with that one."

"I'd like the chance to at least give Plan A a shot," I say. "I've been a hermit for so many years now, the thought of playing hero is all the excitement I have."

"That plan could end up putting you in danger though," #1632 points out like the buzzkill he is. "If the assignment is interfered with, the Big Boss will know. And he will likely discover it was you who made it happen. If he realizes you're still alive, we'll both be executed."

"But I'll be safe, right?" #2007's voice wavers with the question. "I mean, I could just pretend not to know you guys."

"That would probably work, but who knows." He doesn't seem to like my flippancy. "But I guess if you're going to throw logic at me, Plan C is the way to go."

#2007 nods. "In that case, you don't even have to show up at the scene. I can just keep an eye out for the name Victor Franklin and make sure I don't go anywhere near the little girl's wick. Problem solved."

"Oh, no." I shake my head vigorously. "I've been waiting twenty years for this, and I'm damn well going to watch the fruits of my labor."

#1632 raises a hand shyly. "I would also like to witness how this all plays out."

Turning his head, #2007 looks between the two of us. "You don't think you're putting yourselves at risk? Shouldn't you be keeping your head down, Steve? The Big Boss is watching me. He warned me of that."

"The Big Boss isn't watching you on every assignment. Trust me, I know." I take a moment to consider his concerns. He seems like he needs a little handholding and reassurance. "If you keep up with your assignments and quotas until the time comes and work hard to blend in with the others, the Big Boss will have no reason to peep in on you."

"And if he does and he catches you at the scene?" #2007 presses.

I spread my hands. "That's a risk I'm willing to take." Rubbing at the gray scruff on my chin, I add, "Besides, I'm not as recognizable as I was twenty years ago. The Big Boss is used to unchanging faces. Even if he sees me now, there's a real chance he might not recognize me at all."

"You have aged," #1632 adds helpfully.

"Thank you, I'm aware."

#2007 is skeptical as he looks between us. "You really think the Big Boss wouldn't recognize you?"

"Trust me, old friend," I clap a hand on his shoulder, "the big, bad boss isn't as great as he wants everyone to believe. And he doesn't hold nearly as much power as he lets on."

Both of my skeletal friends seem to contemplate this for a moment. Then, #2007 asks, "Who does hold the power?"

It's a question none of us have an answer to, and it hangs stagnant in the air for quite some time. With someone like the Big Boss at the throne, I wonder if any Reaper ever thought there might be someone stronger above even him.

Finally, I shake my head and put the three of us back on track. "Doesn't matter. We're on a mission and that's all I care about. I know we can trust you, #2007." Extending my hand, he accepts it for another handshake. The pumping of our clasped hands is much more confident this time. "It'll be a great pleasure to see this thing through to the end."

#2007 nods as he drops his arm back to his side. "I hope this works out for you, Steve."

So do I, because sparing Heather from a lifetime of fear is the only thing keeping me going now. After the accident, what will I live for next? I genuinely don't know, and I can't admit that out loud to anyone. When my ultimate goal is complete, there will be nothing left for me, and facing that reality is terrifying.

REAPER #2311

Blood pools at my sandaled feet but it doesn't stain the woven straw. The man sprawled on the hardwood floor in front of me is missing the majority of his face. A shotgun lies at an angle beside him, just out of reach of his outstretched hand. The blast knocked it out of his grip, but that doesn't really matter. He got the job done.

I make quick work of severing the man's wick. My scythe has been freshly sharpened, and the blade cuts through the glowing strand like a hot knife through butter. It should be satisfying, but all I feel is a deep sadness for this man who truly believed there was no other way out of his monotonous life. I remind myself that making the final cut is a mercy to him. No doctor in the world could have put the gray matter on the wall back into his shattered skull. Without me, this man would have continued to suffer with unimaginable pain, unable to move his body or cry out for help. His life would be nothing but agony until one of us Reapers came along to relieve him.

I can't look at him anymore, so I hike my scythe up over my shoulder and walk out through the closed door. It's mid-month already, and I've only managed two Random Deaths for my quota. If I don't start killing soon, the Big Boss will take notice, and I can't have that.

Life at Reaper HQ has been lonely without #4821, but my resolve to separate myself from the other killing machines is strong. I haven't spoken a word since his execution. My only company is my own thoughts. No one has noticed.

As I walk the streets of whatever city my assignment landed me in, I keep one eye out for a potential candidate for my quota and let my mind wander. I'm no longer sure how long it's been since I woke up at Headquarters in a daze. I stopped counting the days long ago. The Reapers around me seem perfectly content with the fate they've been handed. I listen to locker room talk of exciting deaths, creative solutions to boring kills, and eagerness over large-scale assignments. I have no doubt that most of the Reapers at HQ were once cold-blooded killers. In which case, the afterlife they've been handed is perfectly suited to them. But there have to be others like me and #4821 out there, too. We can't possibly be the only ones. The problem is, seeking them out would be far too risky. I've accepted that I'm doomed to suffer alone.

A man on the sidewalk shivers as I pass through him, and he looks over his shoulder, searching for the source of the chill. It happens sometimes, when I'm caught up in my own thoughts and I don't instinctively step out of the way of oncoming foot traffic. Not all of the humans feel something when I pass through, though.

For a second, I home in on this man. He's young, much younger than I would ever consider taking as a Random, but I occasionally make exceptions when incurable diseases are at play. But this man is clean, and I let him pass without a second thought.

As I continue my aimless meandering, the city blocks give way to a more suburban area. The homes grow larger and more spaced out. Businesses on street corners cater to a wealthier populace. In the distance, a squat nursing home looms on the horizon. Its well-maintained lawn is immaculate with trimmed hedges and classic wooden picnic tables where the residents can sit and visit with friends and family members.

A sinking relief weighs down the hollowness in my chest. It's not ideal. No Random Death is. But a place like this is better than nothing.

Bypassing the chatter on the sprawling lawn, I enter the building and roam the halls. Several of the residents' doors are open, and I peek into rooms as I walk. Some are empty, some contain people watching TV or sitting with a friend. I scan wicks as I pass by. Some are surprisingly long given the age of its owner; others are so short they are barely flickering with that ethereal blue light anymore.

I have to be careful in a place like this. If I choose too many victims based on the length of their wick, the Big Boss might catch on. I don't know what he would do to me if he did. Some of these residents might also already be on a Reaper's assignment docket, and my slicing of their wick could be seen as interference. I absolutely can't have that.

But I don't feel like ending the life of someone who has plenty of time left if not for my cut. Every time I watch a nice, long wick disintegrate into nothingness, the heavy burden of guilt only becomes stronger in the place where I once had a heart. I really don't know how much more of this I can take.

Finally, near the end of the hall, I come across another open door and poke my skull inside. The TV is on with the volume so low it's barely audible, even to my fine-tuned hearing. A woman named Hattie Mayfield naps in the narrow bed, snoring quietly with one hand gently gripping the safety bar pulled up at her side. Her wick, only about an inch in length, flickers in an invisible breeze.

Perfect.

If I focus too long on her, I will learn more about this woman than I ever want to know. It's better for me if I slice and run, so as few details invade my skull as possible. I don't want to know how many grandchildren she has, or who the great love of her life was. I can't know.

Amping myself up, I rush to her bed, hover my scythe over her curly gray hair, and pull the blade through the wick. It snaps off. Her chest falls and stills. I dash from the room and slump against the hallway wall as if to catch my breath.

A blue flash appears before my eye sockets, and a piece of paper with a pen attached floats down. I hate these stupid report sheets almost as much as I hate the Random Deaths themselves, but they must be filled out. Pressing the paper against the wall for support, I mark in my answers to the completely unnecessary questions.

REAPER #2311

RANDOM DEATH REPORT SHEET

NAME OF EXECUTED: _HATTIE MAYFIELD_

REASON FOR EXECUTION: _CHOSEN RANDOMLY,_
LIKE I'M SUPPOSED TO

METHOD OF EXECUTION: _DRIFTING AWAY IN_
HER SLEEP

I almost don't fill out the reason for execution space. If I were to
get in trouble for leaving it black, I could probably pretend it had
been an accident. But I don't want to risk it, so I take my time with
the whole form before tossing it back up into the air and watching it
disappear in another flash of blue. No one seems to understand the
point of these report sheets, but everyone fills them out anyway. It's
all part of the process.

Picking up my scythe, I pause to admire the way the fluorescent
lights overhead reflect on the blade. The flash of blinding white
against the cool metal is almost enticing, in a way. I wonder, do
Reapers also have wicks? Is there some other being that we can't see
who comes to make the cut when it's our time to crumble to dust?
Where does the cycle start, and where does it end?

I shudder as I run a bony finger along the blade. I feel nothing,
but I like to imagine it hurts; like the sharp sting of a papercut slicing
through layers of skin. When I pull my finger back, I'm shocked to
find a mark on the bone where I made contact with the blade. It

never occurred to me that I could physically harm myself with my own scythe. Somehow, I thought all Reapers were just immune to damage. After all, we're already dead. What's the point of being able to get hurt?

What's the point of anything in this twisted world, really?

Unsure of what to do with this newly discovered knowledge, I tap my scythe on the ground and head back to HQ.

REAPER #1632

The golf course is littered with middle-aged men swinging clubs like scythes. They send balls flying through the air in white blurs and cheer when they land close enough to the hole in the ground to warrant a celebration.

I watch from the sidelines of the 8th hole as a group of friends in colorful plaid shorts make their way through the course. I've been watching their game since the beginning, observing their banter and jeering. My sights are particularly set on the man dressed in shades of pale blue. His wick is noticeably shorter than the ones shooting up from his friends' heads, and the longer I peek into his psyche, the more I can see the hardened clots of plaque clogging the arteries around his struggling heart.

His face is a mottled red as he trails behind his friends, wiping streams of sweat from his brow, and I hear each irregular beat of his heart as it works overtime to deliver blood to his organs. If I leave him be, he'll live another six months before he ends up on some Reapers assignment sheet. Having those six months would probably mean something to this man, but I only have one more victim to fill my quota for the month, and I am determined to get it done today.

He swings his club. He and his friends shield the sun from their eyes and squint as they try to find the little white ball soaring through the air. To everyone's surprise, myself included, the ball plops into the hole with a clattering sound, and the man and his friends erupt into cheers of excitement and disbelief.

A hole in one. What a victory! And this kind of excitement is far too much for a man with such a weak and clogged-up heart.

I am not taking much away from this man. I remind myself of this as I stride over to the celebrating group. Either way, he will be dead soon enough. In the grand scheme of it all, it matters not if I interfere today or if his name ends up in an envelope on my desk in six months' time.

The slice is clean, and he drops to his knees surrounded by his friends. Their excitement shifts to concern with lightning speed. One friend has already pulled a bulky cellular phone from his pocket and is calling for an ambulance. They'll miss him.

I take a few steps back as I accept my report sheet and lower myself down to sit on the grass. Using my knobby knees as a makeshift writing surface, I fill out the form.

REAPER #1632

RANDOM DEATH REPORT SHEET

NAME OF EXECUTED: _Curtis Kovac_

REASON FOR EXECUTION: _Hole-in-one_

METHOD OF EXECUTION: _Heart attack_

Short, sweet, and to the point. I have no need to write an essay for the clerical Reapers. I doubt these reports mean anything anyway.

Sirens wail in the distance, and I settle back on the grass to watch Curtis's body get hauled away by unhurried EMTs who have accepted there is nothing that can be done for a man who's already dead. A nice breeze whips the grass around my skeletal legs, and I imagine the sensation would tickle if I had the nerves to feel such a thing. Steven Kelton must have driven himself mad with thoughts like these, but the more I think about them, the more I see the appeal. There's something to remembering the little sensations that once made us human. It fills me with a strange sense of nostalgia.

Tilting my head up, I watch cottony wisps of clouds float lazily across the bright blue sky. The sun is a white orb that beats down on top of my head, and I lower my hood as if I could actually feel its warmth on my skull. It's nice to pretend, even if dwelling on such non-feelings produces a heaviness on my shoulders that roots me to the ground.

The ambulance leaves, and the man's friends exit the course, but I continue to watch as another round of golfers make their way to the hole, oblivious of the death that just occurred here. They line up their balls and swing their clubs, commenting on the strength of the breeze and the direction from which it comes. There must be a certain science to this sport.

As I watch, a blue flash appears at my side, and I crane my neck to find #2007 standing in the grass beside me.

"There you are," he says.

I spread my hands. "Here I am."

He pulls an envelope from the pocket of his robe. "It's time."

STEVE

Months pass and I become nothing short of a true recluse. I don't leave the house for fear of not being here when my Reaper friends show up on the big day. I pay the neighbor kid to do my grocery shopping and don't sign up for any summer courses at the community center. We're so close to the end now, and I'm not jeopardizing that. Not after all the time I've spent just waiting around.

My days are spent clicking away at my keyboard, but I'm not able to produce anything of value. The anxiety building up with each passing day seems to prevent any decent writing from coming out of my brain. I tend to spend a few hours every day writing slowly, a few words per minute at best, and end up erasing everything I did the next morning. It's almost become a habit at this point. I don't know why I bother stringing together these semi-coherent sentences at all.

When the blue flash comes, I'm so wired I spring up from the couch before the Reapers can fully materialize in the room. My laptop clatters onto the carpet and the screen separates from the keyboard, but I couldn't possibly care less about such a trivial thing.

"Is today the day?" I ask, already heading for the door.

"Yes," #2007 confirms, and a strange sense of disbelief washes over me. After all these years, it's finally time, and I can hardly bring myself to believe it.

"Where?"

"He's going to merge onto Highway 50, heading west, from West State Street. That's where his vehicle will be struck," #2007 says.

I nod and pull my car keys from my pocket. "When?"

#2007 tilts his head and looks at the clock hanging above my TV. "About half an hour."

"Good, that's not far from here."

Leading my otherworldly friends to the garage, I pull open my car doors and gesture for them to get inside.

#1632 pauses, studying the vehicle with a hint of skepticism radiating off him. "Will this work?"

"Don't worry, I've done it before," I say, and swat his bony frame into the backseat while #2007 takes shotgun without question. "I would say but buckle up, but..." I trail off, chuckling at my own joke as I hop into the driver's seat and secure the seatbelt over my torso.

The car roars to life, and I ease it down the driveway. I have this town's layout memorized from the main highway to all the tiny, potholed backroads. After moving here, I made it my mission to explore every nook and cranny of this place, and I make the turns carefully while making sure to keep my speed right at the legal limit. Can't have any traffic stops or accidents of our own on a day like today.

A few minutes later, I pull off the road and park a few hundred feet away from where West State Street merges onto Highway 50. I'm not sure what exactly I'm going to do to prevent this accident, but I figure I'll know when the time comes. Coming up with plans on the fly hasn't let me down so far.

Once I've helped the Reapers out of the car, we head for the intersection. My watch says we have about five more minutes until showtime, and I know they're about to be the longest five minutes of my life. Even longer than the twenty years I've spent waiting for this exact moment.

#2007's skull swivels as he surveys the area. "If you want to watch from the sidewalk, I'll just—"

"I'm going to give Plan A a shot first," I announce, and they both come to a screeching halt.

"Steven Kelton," #1632 begins, "we agreed that your Plan C, which frankly should have been Plan A from the beginning, was the best course of action."

I hold up my hands and take in a slow breath. "Look, I've been thinking a lot about this, and I really want to try to stop the accident. Isn't it worth it to at least try to give Heather a life with her father?"

"I'll be caught!" #2007 protests.

"Blame it on me. I've thought that through, too. I knew it was going to happen, and I meddled in the affairs of the Reapers all on my own. Simple."

"And what of me?" #1632 asks. Although his face is only a permanently smiling skull, I feel the weight of his glare on me. "The Big Boss will know I did not really execute you."

"Claim ignorance," I say, throwing my hands up. "I'm already an enigma. Maybe you cut my wick, left, and I just got right back up again. For all the Big Boss knows, coming back has made me immortal. There's a way for you to get out of this too." I'm growing desperate now. All I want is to do as much for Heather as I possibly can.

They exchange a look, a silent conversation passing between them.

Finally, #2007 lets out an exasperated sigh. "Fine, do it. It's not going to work anyway."

"You have so little faith in me."

#1632 shifts on his feet. "You have not led me astray yet, Steven Kelton. If you really feel you must try, I shall support your decision." His words are hollow, and I'm sure deep down he agrees with #2007. "But tell me, what exactly do you plan to do to stop this accident?"

"Well," I hesitate, "I'm not quite sure about that yet. It's kind of hard to plan when I didn't even know where it was going to happen. Now that I do, I can really think it through."

"And you have about two minutes to do it," #2007 says more to himself than to me.

These Reapers really don't have much confidence in me. And after all I've been through, too.

With a huff of defiance, I scan the surrounding area and am struck with what can only be described as a stroke of genius. My finger shoots out, and the two death machines follow my pointing digit to the crosswalk. "He'll have to slow down for a pedestrian!" I cry, and dart across the grass to the sidewalk.

#2007 scoffs at my back, and I hear him mutter to #1632, "We'll see how fast this falls apart."

I don't see it, but I imagine #1632 is nodding. Rude. But it's the best I've got. And if I don't have confidence in myself, who will? Clearly not these two.

I reach the sidewalk and jab the button to cross several times for good measure. Bouncing from foot to foot, I look up the road and catch sight of a navy-blue minivan approaching. #2007 and #1632 have joined me, flanking either side of my body, which is buzzing with anticipation.

"That's him," #2007 confirms, his tone grim. His finger bones tighten around his scythe. He wants to prevent this useless death just as much as I do, but he's become jaded. I can't blame him. Working as a corporate killing machine can do that.

Looking up, I find the streetlight still green, the little man on the crosswalk sign still a bright, blaring red. My knees bend, ready to burst forth. I jab the button again. The stupid thing is probably a placebo, but I have to try. I have to do something. Even if it means jaywalking. I'll do it. For her. I have to. She'll never know, but I owe her everything.

The van approaches. The stoplight flashes yellow. I step onto the crosswalk.

The van doesn't slow. The light turns red. I take another step, my eyes glued to the old vehicle with rust blooming at the seams. It still maintains its speed.

Through the windows, I can see it. A little girl in a booster seat, Heather, kicking and screaming. Tugging at her seatbelt. Shouting words through spit-shiny lips that I can't hear. Tears wetting chubby cheeks. A tantrum. A full-blown, child-sized tantrum. And Victor Franklin doesn't see me on the crosswalk because he has twisted around in the driver's seat and is attempting to soothe his child.

A good father. A confident driver. A dangerous combination.

I step backward onto the sidewalk just in time for the van to plow through the intersection and crumple against a sedan who was obeying their traffic signal. Both vehicles spin out, tires tracing stinking black marks onto the road. The van careens to the side like a skateboard trick and tips over. The sedan's front is forced onto the sidewalk across from me. The middle-aged driver emerges with a look of bewilderment, dazed but miraculously unharmed, although I imagine he'll be sore tomorrow.

As for Victor Franklin...

I turn my head, forcing myself to look despite the burning bile rising into the back of my throat. The child's defiant screams have turned to cries of pain, anguish, and fear. They swell like a macabre symphony through the shattered windshield. Bright afternoon sunlight beats down on the van, giving me a perfect view of Victor Franklin and his blood-drenched face. The seatbelt, probably old and slightly frayed, snapped with the force of the impact, and his skull is indented at the temple where it slammed into the window. Glass shards protrude from his left eye. It seems he tried to turn back around, only to face the onslaught of death head-on. Had he remained focused on his child, at least he would have had something beautiful to look at in the end.

Everything sounds like it's underwater until #1632 grips my bare arm with his cold, bony fingers. Then the sounds roll back in, forcing me to acknowledge reality. My ass hits the curb as I sit down hard, the shockwave forced up my spine a minor, faraway nuisance.

"Holy hell, did you get lucky, man."

Looking up, I find a young man, probably a college student, standing beside me. His long hair is swept up in the light breeze, exposing just enough of his face for me to see the wrinkles of concern on his forehead. Was he waiting to cross too? I never registered that another person was even there. I don't say anything. I can't.

"You looked like you were in a hurry, too," he continues, a tremble in his voice. "That would have killed you, man. Those reflexes kicked in just in time."

His hand goes to my shoulder. I feel it shaking. Still, I stare dumbly at the intersection. Everything confined within those four points seems to be frozen. Nothing moves. Even Heather's wails have died down.

"You just relax, man," the young man continues as he takes a few steps back. "I'm going to find a phone. Get an ambulance." He pauses. "You don't happen to have a cell, do you?"

I shake my head, my neck so stiff I can hear the muscles creak deep inside my ears.

"Damn. Okay, you just relax. Would've shit myself if I were you."

He takes off running then, fueled by the adrenaline brought on by his own brush with death. He'll probably be feeling all that and then some later.

"Steve," #2007 says from beside me. "Steve, I have to cut the wick. I have to. He's suffering."

I don't say anything. All this time wasted. All these years spent for nothing. I couldn't repay her for everything she's done for me after all. I should have shot myself in the face when I had the chance. It wouldn't have made a difference. The old injury in my right shoulder aches as if to agree.

"Steve," #2007 says again.

"You don't need my permission!" The words spew out with a venom that stings even #2007's nerveless body, and he recoils. "Just do your job."

#2007 hesitates, wanting to say something. I can't imagine what. But he decides against it and turns on his heel, making a beeline for the van, which has begun to leak oil from under the hood.

For a few minutes, #1632 and I watch in silence as #2007 carefully pushes his scythe through the broken glass so he can reach the dying man's wick. Somewhere far in the distance, an ambulance wails. At the very least, Heather is safe. Although I've done nothing to change the course of her life, she's safe. I guess that's the best I can hope for now.

#1632 makes a show of clearing his throat, a ridiculous gesture considering he doesn't even have a throat. "You know what this means, don't you?"

Slowly, I tilt my head and look up at his imposing, black-cloaked form. All of the fight has drained from my body. All of the will. There's nothing there. Uttering the single word takes all I have left. "What?"

#1632 is quiet for a maddeningly long time, like he doesn't want to share his thoughts after all. It doesn't matter much to me if he speaks or not. I can sit on this curb in silence for the rest of my life for all I care now.

Finally, he lowers himself to sit beside me. His eye sockets are trained on his bony knees, making sharp angles against the durable fabric of his robe. "Heather caused the accident."

I hear the words, but their meaning takes longer for me to register. When they do, I suck in a breath so sharp I expect my throat to bleed. "No."

"I am sorry, Steven Kelton."

I shake my head, rapid and jerky movements, as if I could shake away the truth. "She's five. She's a child."

"Her actions directly resulted in someone's death."

"She didn't know what she was doing!" I rise to my feet, fists clenched at my sides, ready to fight. Fight who, though?

#1632?

The Big Boss?

The system?

Who?

And how?

"So many people do not," #1632 says. There's no comfort in his voice. No sympathy. I shouldn't have expected any. At the end of the day, he's nothing but a ruthless killing machine, just like the rest of them. A slave to the system. A cog in the machine.

I've been kidding myself all these years.

My fists unfurl. My vision goes gray at the edges. My knees buckle and I plop back onto the curb. "It's not fair."

"There is no fairness in death," #1632 says, his sage tone grating at my nerves. "You know as well as I do that even accidents—"

I clap my hands against my ears. "Don't say it!"

Two ambulances and a police cruiser come to a stop at the intersection. EMTs spill out and assess the situation. A fat officer who can't seem to keep his pants up saunters over to the driver of the sedan for a statement. It's all so routine; so cut and dry. Everyone here will acknowledge that this little girl's life will be changed forever, but they don't know just how much. They couldn't know.

#2007 rejoins us on the curb, his head bent down. He takes in the look on my face and pulls his scythe to his chest like a teddy bear. "What's wrong? I know this didn't exactly go as planned, but..."

#1632 offers a slow shake of the head. "That little girl has condemned herself to the life of a Reaper."

I slam my fist against the rough concrete and stand. My car might as well be miles away with the way I'm feeling, but I go to it anyway. My otherworldly companions don't bother to follow. That's fine by me. Our mission failed. It's over. I have no use for them anymore and they have no use for me. Might as well come clean to the Big Boss. We can all lose our heads. What does it matter?

Sliding into the passenger seat and gripping the steering wheel, I see that my knuckles are smeared with blood. The sight of the injury brings forth a dull ache, and I welcome the pain with open arms. At least I'm feeling something.

For a while, I do nothing but sit and breathe. Breathe and sit. That policeman probably wanted to get a statement from me. I was a witness, after all. But what could I possibly say to him? That a little five-year old girl has unwittingly doomed herself to become a ruthless killer when her time in her human body is up? That that made sense all along but I was too stupid, too naïve, and too unwilling to believe to actually admit it?

I changed my fate, but I can't change hers. What, then, was the point? I wanted a second chance, and I got it. Somehow, I got it. But I've wasted it. I've done nothing of value, and now I know I never will. My one goal failed spectacularly, and there's nothing I can do to fix it. I can change my fate, but I can't change destiny. She is a ruthless bitch.

What the hell am I supposed to do now?

Slowly, I bend down, press my forehead into the steering wheel, and scream.

REAPER #2311

It's been months. The chip on my fingerbone from my scythe hasn't healed. I've managed to scar myself and somehow, it feels good. Like a step in the right direction, although I still don't know where I'm going.

I keep my head low. I do the assignments that appear on my desk. I complete my monthly quotas in an acceptable, timely manner. And through it all, I block everything out. The office chatter, the pride, the blood. It's the only way I can stay sane around here.

Every day, I'm consumed by the thought of getting out. But how? That's where I'm stuck. There are only two ways I know of for sure: waiting until I crumble to dust, which could be hundreds of years off, or by the Big Boss's blade.

This thought gives me pause as I sit at my desk, waiting for the next envelope to drop through the labyrinth of pipes that crisscross the ceiling in a giant, tangled web. My focus shifts to that little nick in my finger bone. I did that with my own scythe. I can hurt myself.

Yes.

I can hurt myself.

And if I can hurt myself, then...

Then what? What would happen if I were to take my execution into my own hands, sentence myself to death and do the job myself? What's waiting on the other side?

The thought sends a hard chill through my skeleton, and my teeth chatter together with the force of it.

What if it's nothing?

What if it's something?

Something, anything better than this.

I can't possibly know, and I'm doubtful that anyone around here does. Even if they did, they wouldn't tell me.

But maybe I could find out. There has to be something somewhere in this vast headquarters of death. Some secret, some tome, some clue. This can't be the end of it all. It just can't. I won't accept that. I can take matters into my own hands and find out for myself.

As my mind races with these thoughts, an envelope drops from above and lands with grace on my desktop. My mind clears and I tear it open as I stand, ready to complete the death assigned to me. Because, in the end, I'm nothing but a coward.

REAPER #1632

The return to headquarters is completed in silence. #2007 keeps his skull tilted down, his eye sockets trained on the floor as we roam the hallway side-by-side. Other Reapers shuffle past, some on their way to the Transportation Room, others heading for a hot cup of Elixir and a well-deserved break.

I don't know where #2007 and I are going, but we continue our aimless walk until he finally stops and speaks, his voice so low I must strain to make sense of the words.

"We should have gone after him."

His tone is laden with guilt, and I slump against the wall. A quick glance around confirms that, for the time being, it's just the two of us occupying this vast, stretching hall somewhere between the rarely used courtroom and the filing room.

"There is nothing any of us could have done to prevent what happened. We know that now, and Steven Kelton needs time to accept that."

"He waited so long—"

"None of us could have known," I remind him, and his shoulders slump.

"Do you really think Heather was always destined to be a Reaper?" #2007 asks, defeated.

I take a moment to ponder the question. Steven Kelton managed to change his timeline – an unheard-of feat. But that doesn't mean he can change anyone else's. Destiny, fate, free will, whatever one may call it, lies only in the hands of the individual. Only they have the power to make a change, and one cannot expect a child to have that kind of awareness.

"I suppose," I finally say.

#2007 looks down, his fingers toying with his robe. "It seems cruel. Unfair. She didn't mean it."

"Very few people mean anything they do. Humans are creatures of impulse."

"I suppose you've been around long enough to know," #2007

mumbles.

I sense the shift in #2007, the sinking feeling of defeat. If he continues down this path, the Big Boss will undoubtedly take notice. He is already on thin ice. With another glance around the stretching hall to ensure its vacancy, I reach out and place a hand on the young Reaper's shoulder. "Heed my advice. Forget Steven Kelton. Forget second chances. Whatever happened to him won't happen to either of us. Somehow, he managed to override the system. In the end, he just got lucky. Forget it. All of it. Push it aside and focus only on your work. Keep your head down and do what's asked of you."

"Until the day I crumble to dust." #2007 says the part I do not.

I nod. "One way or another, we have all earned this fate. Pay your penance, and then, perhaps, true freedom awaits."

"Pay my penance," he repeats with a scoff, shaking his skull with a slow, deliberate motion. "I don't even remember what I'm paying for. Do you?"

"It does not matter." My answer is instant, automatic. I will not let the question worm its way into my mind. It will only consume me. I will not become a fearful, sniveling shell of a Reaper desperate to find a way out.

Holding up a hand, I note the tiny cracks forming on my yellowing fingerbones. I wonder just how much time I have left.

The silence hangs. #2007 keeps his spine pressed against the damp stone wall, eye sockets trained on the floor. After some time, he ventures to speak once more.

"I can't just forget him. We should check up on him, make sure he's okay. He spent all that time planning, waiting, for nothing. There has to be something we can do."

"Forget it now," I instruct him, a firmness in my voice. "We have no reason to have anything else to do with Steven Kelton."

"He's our friend!" #2007 cries, his voice echoing dangerously down the long, dim hall.

I stare at #2007's blank skull, feeling the desperation seeping out of his bones, imagining the twisted look that would be etched into his facial features if he had any. Then, slowly, I shake my head. He must learn the hard truths about life in this place. "Reapers do not have friends."

STEVE

I don't know how long I sit in my car, forehead pressed to the steering wheel, blood dripping onto the floor from my knuckles, throat raw from screaming, but it's dark when I finally lift my head and blink, bleary-eyed at the row of streetlights illuminating the road in front of me. In the rearview mirror, I catch sight of my tear-soaked face, a thick red line marking my forehead. In the back of my mind, I register my stomach growling. Some primal instinct reminds me that I have to eat. Have to drink. Have to sleep.

My mouth feels full of cotton, my eyelids heavy. Mechanically, I take care of one need at a time, letting my body slip into autopilot as I grab a burger and soda from the drive thru and wolf it down on my way home. Leaving my car in the garage, I stumble into the house and fall into bed without bothering to change. What's the point? What's the point of anything? Why did I even bother eating? Everything was for nothing. Everything was wasted. I'm a waste. I should have stayed a Reaper. Played along like a good little killing machine. I should have allowed myself to transform into an emotionless husk and carried out my assignments until the day I became nothing but ash in a janitorial Reaper's dustpan.

But no. I had to go and fight for something new, something different, something I didn't even know I should be fighting for. And now look at me. A failure in death, a failure in life. Nothing but a failure.

I bury my face into my pillow with thoughts of smothering in my sleep and drift off.

To my dismay, I wake up in the morning groggy and half-convinced the previous day had been nothing but a horrible nightmare. But my wrinkled, unchanged clothes confirm that the bad dream was reality, and my heart sinks so far into my stomach I can no longer hear its rhythmic beating in my chest.

I sit up, swinging my legs over the edge of the bed, but I can't manage any more than that. I wonder if I'll ever be able to.

Thoughts swirl in my mind on an endless loop. What now? No

purpose. What now? No purpose. What now? No purpose. Over and over and over again.

There's the community center, I suppose. But those classes were only a way to bide my time, to give me something to do until the big day arrived.

What, I wonder, would I have done had the plan succeeded, though? It occurs to me now that I'd probably be in the same place I am now. No more waiting, no more purpose, mission accomplished. What would I have done? What would be different?

I guess I could move back to Indiana, take the reigns back on my company and no longer be a silent partner. But going back to corporate life sounds awful.

So, what now?

Heather is doomed. My life no longer has meaning. The thing I waited so long for finally happened, and what a bust that was! Now, I guess, the only thing I have left to wait for is the day a Reaper comes to take a whack at my wick. I could make it easy on them. With the past twenty years completely wasted, I have to admit the thought is enticing.

Somehow, while lost in the thought, the hollow pit in my stomach guides me to the kitchen. Some other Steve puts slices of bread into the toaster, butters them, and adds a generous dollop of grape jelly. This other Steve is also kind enough to start the coffee maker. Just another day for the neighborhood recluse.

With the meager breakfast eaten and the hollow space temporarily filled, I drift into the living room. My eyes fall to the laptop, resting broken on the carpet. Without thinking, I pick it up, set it on the coffee table, and plug the charger in. To my surprise, the screen, hanging on to the keyboard by a few thin wires and cracked plastic, illuminates. Maybe not all is lost after all. I couldn't save Heather. I have no desire to return to bossing others around. But there is one thing left that I'm good at. One person left to live for, even if she's no longer here to cheer me on.

I pull up my latest project – a full-length novel I've been toying around with for the past few years, more concept than actual plot for the time being. After scanning the last few sentences I wrote, I poise my fingers over the keyboard and begin to type.

At least it's something.

REAPER #2311

With my assignments finished for the day and my quota fulfilled, I duck out of the breakroom and venture into the vast, winding hallways that make up Reaper HQ. Although I'm not quite sure what I'm looking for, I know I'm not going to find it in the well-traveled, heavily populated areas of the corporate office. Every company has secrets, and I want to dig up something that will get me out of here one way or another. On my own terms.

Past the cubicles, beyond the courtroom where I pause only to shudder at the memory of #4821's unfair demise, and bypassing the filing room, I find myself in a long, stretching hallway. While this one is identical to all the others, with its limestone walls, smooth floors, and the sound of dripping water coming from everywhere and nowhere all at once, the emptiness sets it apart. A creeping, blackish-green mold snakes over the ground, its progress uninterrupted by the tread of footsteps.

The eternal flames in the sconces lining the dewy walls have, ironically, gone out, and the black hole before me creates the illusion of an endless tunnel. Something akin to fear pulls at me, warning me to step back, turn around, leave well enough alone. But I've come this far. I'm not going to stop now. If I end up lost, wandering a maze of black halls, unable to see for the rest of my pitiful time here, then so be it. At least I won't have to kill anymore.

Reaching out to my side, I press my hand flat against the stone wall. Although I have no nerves to actually feel the dampness, the hardness, just knowing something physical is there is enough to ground me, and I take one determined step into the dark.

It shrouds me like a thick blanket blocking out the sun. One moment, I'm able to perceive my surroundings. The next, nothing.

I take another step.

Another.

Another.

I don't know how I long I walk within the purest black with only my hand on the wall to remind me that I haven't been swallowed by the void. I lost count of my steps around the two-hundred mark. But I continue to press forward. Waiting to hit a wall that marks a turn or a dead end, anticipating a change in my surroundings, something. Anything.

And then, suddenly, up ahead, a glimpse of light. Nothing but a thin strip illuminating patches of algae and shallow puddles on a floor that appears dipped and mottled from overuse.

A door! It has to be. The light spills from the gap between it and the floor, dim but perceivable. I take my hand from the wall and rush toward it, my skeleton warming with a sense of hope. For what, exactly, I can't imagine. But it's there.

When the light hits my sandals, I pause. I can't let my excitement overshadow caution. Yes, this is definitely a door in front of me, although it has no knob or handle, with an ancient word much like the squiggles and scrawls emblazoned on the Big Boss's office door carved into the bloated wood. But anything could be on the other side, and I have to be prepared for just that.

Purely out of habit, I force a long inhale through the hole that was once covered by a fleshy nose. The whistling sound the gesture produces echoes down the hallway at a near deafening volume, and I cut off the unnecessary breath with a sense of panic tightening my jaw. Statue still, I strain my sense of hearing and listen. The whistle fades out somewhere far, far away. The faint sound of running water somewhere further down the hall registers within me, and I make a mental note to check it out later. But first, the door.

I lean forward with caution, pressing the side of my skull against the softened wood. All is quiet within.

Just to be safe, I tap my fingers against the door, ready to duck into the safety of the darkness should something shift on the other side. But no sound comes.

Steeling myself, I place both hands on the door and push. It doesn't budge. I try again, throwing my shoulder into it as well and feeling it sink a little against the moisture-damaged wood.

With a grunt of frustration, I take a step back and examine the barrier. The only way in is through, and I didn't come this far to give up now. Besides, I'm dying to know what's on the other side, no pun intended. Some primal, childish curiosity is all but demanding I find a way in.

There's only one option, really. I have to take a moment to hype myself up, but once I'm ready, I tilt my skull down and run full speed into the door. A semi-human battering ram. The force of the blow knocks my head back, and my spine creaks in protest, but the door pushes inward a few centimeters, and ancient hinges scream out in surprise.

It's not much, but it's progress.

This time, I back up until my spine hits the wall opposite the door. I lower my head once more and collide with the wood. The hinges squeal and groan, and the heavily swollen wood fights with the stone doorframe, but after five good, hard rammings, the door flies open and I go sprawling onto the floor, arms and legs splayed, washed in an orange light.

For a few minutes, I'm too stunned to move. I can only lie prostrate on the damp stone, lightheaded and vision swirling. Slowly, my right hand goes to the top of my skull, and I'm surprised to find little chips of bone missing, much like the nick on my finger. I've really been doing a number on myself lately.

Shakily, I rise to my feet and pull my arms against my chest.

My skull swivels as I take in the walls lined with bookshelves, stuffed with bloated, water-damaged tomes. It takes a moment for me to even fully register what I'm looking at. The only book I've ever seen within this corporation of death is the Rule Book, which sits under a glass dome on a pedestal in the Big Boss's office. But this is a library. An actual library.

The room is smaller than I would have expected. A wooden table that appears ready to disintegrate at the slightest touch sits squarely in the middle. Six chairs in various states of decomposition surround it. On the wall, flanking either side of the door, hang two torches, their eternal flames dim but still going strong.

I'm reminded of a designated study space in a university library. I once killed a man on an east coast college campus in a space alarmingly similar to this. An aneurysm had burst within his brain. Quick and painless. He faceplanted into an open book of Greek mythology, which he was diligently studying for a paper he had to write. He was behind on the deadline. I remember feeling his worry, which was nearing panic, as I cut the wick. Although it was an Assigned Death, I like to think I spared him from being reprimanded for a late assignment.

A library.

I force my thoughts back to the present. Was this room also once used as some sort of space to study? But to study what, exactly? Methods of killing? Reaper etiquette? What else is there in a place like this?

The floor is slick with stagnant water, and I walk carefully to the wall-to-wall, floor-to-ceiling shelves. There must be at least a thousand books here, but they all appear to be so damaged, I wonder if anything inside them is legible. Still, I have to know.

My eye sockets fall on a leather-bound volume in a rich, forest green. Remnants of gold embossing still adorn the spine, although most of it has flaked off with its age, leaving only hollow pits to highlight where the title should be. The leather is so worn, the words are illegible.

Turning it carefully in my hands, I take a moment to examine the cover. No dice. It's the same. I don't expect the inside to be any better, but just in case, I peel open the thick pages and find the scrawling of the ancient language. Pages and pages. Handwritten. Faded black ink on crinkled papyrus. Disappointment clouds my vision, and I allow the book to slip from my hands. It lands at my feet, closing with a snap of finality. The water ripples with the disturbance. I know I should be more careful. This is an extraordinary find, every book an anthropologic wonder. But what good do they do if no one can read them?

I make my way along the shelf, pulling books at random and finding nothing but those squiggles within. Whoever wrote these damn books didn't even bother to include a helpful illustration or two. Just pages and pages of words no one can read. No wonder this place has fallen into disuse. I don't think even the oldest Reapers here can read the ancient language.

I grow more and more discouraged as I work my way along the shelves, cracking books open, ignoring the creaks of protest from the leather, and scanning a page or two before shoving them haphazardly back into place. This can't be the end of the line. It just can't. There has to be something here; something within these hundreds of thousands of pages.

When I've wrapped my way around the shelves and get to the last few rows beside the entrance, I notice a shift. The unreadable squiggles are beginning to grow more uniform, and they look close to the Roman alphabet I've learned to read. Not quite, but close. Almost. A fluttering sensation unleashes in my chest cavity, and I grab the next bound tome with a renewed sense of excitement. While still unreadable, I can make out the beginnings of the modern English alphabet. Maybe this little field trip was worth it after all.

Wedged between two flaming red covers, a black-bound book sticks out slightly, as if its previous reader had been in a rush and hadn't had the time or patience to push it back in flush with the other books. I reach for it, entertaining the idea of discovering some great secret within these pages. If, that is, I can even read them.

Like all the others, the cover is distorted. Dry, brittle flakes of cracking leather break free and settle around my feet. If words were once printed on this cover, they're long gone now. Slowly, so as not to do any further damage, I open the book. The spine has gone stiff, and the disturbance causes the leather to crack with the sound of a thunderclap. More flakes fall to the floor. But the book is open.

The title page is smudged and water stained, but the red-inked words still stand out on the yellowed paper.

Ain Guidæ ophe Reapĕr Reformacion

Still not quite the English I was hoping for, but at least I can read it. Although I don't know the meaning of a couple of the words, there are a few I definitely know. Guide. Reaper. Reformation. Could this be...?

I stare at the words. For how long, I don't know. The tip of my fingerbone traces each letter one-by-one, as if assuring myself they're really there. Some kind of guide for the reformation of Reapers. Reformation as in rehabilitation? Who is this for?

With caution, I turn on my heel and lower the book onto the splintered tabletop. Once I'm sure it will hold, I grab the sturdiest-looking chair and pull it up. Lowering my bony frame into the seat, I take a long moment to just look at my discovery, pondering what could possibly be scribed on the brittle pages. Something inside me flickers; a glimmering of hope, excitement, anxiety. A whole slew of wonderful, human emotions so strong it takes me a while to process them individually. But when I do, I find that curiosity is overpowering them all. I so badly want to grin as I dip my finger under the first page and turn it over.

Quickly, a frustration settles over me as I struggle to read the archaic English. Most of the words are maddingly unintelligible to me. The few I can pick out don't make much sense without context. But I grit me teeth and carry on.

There are some illustrations within these pages, to my pleasant surprise, and since I can't read too many of the words, I take my time to carefully study the images.

A full-page piece of artwork that reminds me of a medieval tapestry depicts a looming, yellow-boned Reaper. Its height is accented by the three smaller Reapers who stand beside it at waist-height, and the image reminds me of looking at the Big Boss when he's trying to be intimidating. But the large Reaper is extending its arm in a gesture of welcome. The others appear to be paying apt attention, as if something is being explained.

This can't be the Big Boss I know – if the Reaper shown here is meant to be a Big Boss at all. I've never known our great overseer to take the time to teach anyone. The act is too far below him. But that does appear to be what's happening here.

I've gleaned all I can from this image, and I flip through several more pages until I find another. This painting would have stopped my heart if I had one. A Reaper on its knees, head back, hands pressed to its temples. A human is sprawled before the Reaper, throat slashed, blood seeping to the bottom of the page. A scythe lies in the red puddle. The human's wick has been recently severed.

I may not have a heart, but something deep inside me aches. I can certainly relate to this image. Maybe too well.

My excitement has fizzled with the heaviness portrayed in the picture, and I turn the pages with the slowness of someone feeling the onset of exhaustion. Maybe that is what I'm feeling. Not physically, of course. But mentally. Emotions in general are a heavy burden to bear, but when they whip back and forth at a breakneck pace between the positives and the negatives, it can really take a toll on the psyche. This is probably why Reapers aren't supposed to feel. I wonder what part of the brain-washing process got messed up when I was brought to HQ on that first day.

The flames in the sconces flicker in unison. It may be my imagination, but I think the room grows a little dimmer, too. I may not have much time, and I can't be caught with this outside this room. I'll be executed for sure. So, I flip through a few more pages. The book isn't very long compared to some of the other volumes jammed on the shelf, and soon I'm turning to the final page.

When I do, my instincts take over, and I gasp.

REAPER #1632

Life resumes as normal, although I can't help but notice that #2007 has kept a wary distance between us. Knowing him, I have my doubts that it's for our safety. I do wonder if he's gone to visit Steve since that day, now years behind us. But if he has, it's no business of mine. My only interest now lies in self-preservation.

The Big Boss has called me to inner guard duty for the day – a welcome reprieve. I fear I am beginning to feel my age. My bones have yellowed. A few small cracks have formed at the tips of my fingers and other heavily used areas. The average Reaper doesn't last more than a few hundred years, from what I've gathered. Unless, of course, you are the Big Boss. No one is entirely sure just how old the looming authority over us is, but from listening in to the office gossip, I have gathered that not even the oldest Reapers here remember a time when the Big Boss was not the Big Boss.

Like me, he has also begun to show signs of aging, although I note that his are much more advanced than mine. When I arrived at this place, he was already yellowed, micro-cracks lacing his exposed bone. Now, he hunches forward, his spine arced, as if his back pains him, and it appears to take effort to raise his skull and address any issues that may arrive at his feet. I believe he is trying to hide these deteriorations by increasing the volume of his voice. When he speaks, he sounds more powerful than ever.

To his chagrin, #2007 has also been assigned guard duty today. He stands on the other side of the office door and looks pointedly at anything but me. I wonder how long a Reaper can hold a grudge. Surely, he must realize that I am right. We no longer have anything to do with Steven Kelton, fascinating as he is.

Though I detest myself for admitting it, my thoughts do drift to the human. He must be quite old by now, although I'm unsure exactly how many years have passed since our last encounter. Time has an odd way of melting away in a place like this. But he must still be alive. Had an assignment come through to slice his wick for real, the Big Boss would have surely gotten word on it, and my deception would undoubtedly result in my final death. These days, though, that possibility doesn't seem too terrifying. At least, with my help, the man got to try.

The office is deathly quiet. A sound as small as #2007 tapping his thumb on the handle of his scythe echoes up to the high ceiling, and the Big Boss lifts his head.

"Stop that," he snaps.

#2007 stiffens, and his hand tightens around the weapon's staff. "My apologies, sir." His skull tilts slightly to the side. For a moment, I believe he might be looking at me, but then his gaze shifts to the eternal flame flickering behind my head.

With boredom overtaking me, my mind drifts back to Steven Kelton against my will. Perhaps, I think, I should pay him a visit after all. If only to check the length of his wick. His time left on earth will very likely correlate with my time left at Reaper HQ, and I would like to be prepared.

Just as I begin to plan my social call, the office doors burst open with a force so strong, #2007 and I are both knocked to the ground.

In a daze, I swivel my head around, trying to catch a glimpse of the intruder, but there is no one there. All I see are the two outer guards peering into the room with their jaws hanging in twin expressions of comical surprise.

The Big Boss is on his feet in an instant, his bones creaking as he strides to the middle of the room, fingers balled into fists at his sides. He, too, surveys the room. The red embers deep within his eye sockets flare.

"Who goes there?" he demands, his booming voice bouncing off the ceiling and ricocheting through the vast space.

The silence which follows feels like hours, but only seconds pass before an equally authoritative voice replies. "Good day, Grim Reaper #105. I trust that you are doing well."

As the voice reverberates from everywhere and nowhere all at once, a curious sight fills my eye sockets. A pulsating glow of the most luscious, swirling shades of violet I could ever imagine blinks into view in the middle of the room. Within minutes, a gaseous cloud streaked with electric tendrils of white lightning occupies the space. The shimmers pulsing through the thing's body like a heartbeat remind me of staring into a mug of steaming Elixir.

No one speaks. Then, finally, a chuckle.

"You do not know who I am?" the thing asks, sounding more amused than offended. The streaks of lightning fizzle audibly with each syllable. "I suppose I can't blame you. I've not yet had the opportunity to introduce myself, although your predecessor should have mentioned me."

I realize I am still sitting on the stone floor, legs splayed. Though I have not yet recovered from the initial shock, I scramble to my feet. #2007 follows my example. But from here, neither of us know what to do. Guard duty has never required either of us to actually be a guard before. We exchange a glance, and he shrugs.

The Big Boss, far more occupied with the glowing being before him than his fumbling guards, tucks his chin against his clavicle as he scrutinizes our sudden guest. "What are you, and what business do you have here?"

"I am not a what, but a *who*." The cloud pulsates with indignance. "Forgive my sudden appearance. I am Mrtyu, Regional Manager of the Northern Galactic Branch of Death and Rebirth." The gasses that make up Mrtyu dim as a sound that could only be a sigh swells in the atmosphere. "It sounds so much more poetic in the original language. A shame, really."

The Big Boss straightens his shoulders and rises to his full height. Now there is no trace of the curve developing in his spine. His stature is almost intimating, even to me, who has long ago lost the fear of the presiding authority.

"I have never heard of such a thing," the Big Boss declares, and he slashes his hand through the air as if swatting away a pesky fly. "Leave my office before I have my guards forcefully remove you."

The outer guards have stepped inside to observe the curious scene, and we look at each other with what can only be bemusement. How does he expect us to do that?

Mrtyu chuckles, the gasses inside them twinkling. "As you wish, Grim Reaper #105. However, I should think you'd like to hear the results of your quincentenary review before I depart."

The flaming embers inside the Big Boss's eyes flicker with sudden recognition. "I recall my predecessor receiving a similar review before passing the torch onto me."

"Indeed, my colleague Aeon was the one to execute Grim Reaper #59's performance review. I apologize for not being present that day. Unfortunately, I had a bit of a situation to contend with on Planet Dagon. What a mess that was! Now, let's see here..."

Like a bizarre magic trick, a manilla file blinks into existence, hovering in front of the cloud. It opens of its own accord and the sound of shuffling papers fills the room. The Big Boss still appears skeptical as his arms cross over his broad-ribbed chest.

"Is there a particular reason why this must be done now?"

"Of course." Mrtyu delivers the news with a pleasant tone. "Your five-hundred years are up, Grim Reaper #105. Your review will serve as a basis to pass down to your successor, whomever you may choose, and you will be expected to begin their training as soon as possible. We can't have another incident of the trainer crumbing to dust before the trainee can be fully informed of their duties. Your days are numbered, I'm afraid."

"What?" the Big Boss roars as he puffs up again. However, the menacing act has no effect on Mrtyu. They simply continue sorting through their papers, as if searching for the right one. "I have no intention of giving up my seat!"

"Ah, but you must," Mrtyu says with the practiced tone of someone who has delivered this speech time and time again. "As you may recall, your contract clearly states that after five-hundred years of overseeing the Reapers assigned to Planet Earth, your position, and your lifespan, shall come to an end."

"I remember reading no such thing!" the Big Boss cries, and he takes a surprised step back as an old parchment scroll materializes in his line of vision.

"No one ever reads the fine print," Mrtyu laments, a *tsk*-ing sound echoing throughout the office. "Regardless, it's all there. Take a look for yourself."

The Big Boss doesn't appear to be in any mood to humor the gaseous being, and he batters the scroll out of the way as he takes three long strides up to the space where Mrtyu floats. I didn't think it was possible for a being that's nothing but a cloud of glowing gases and lightning to flinch, but they appear to constrict into themself as the Big Boss approaches.

"I am not done here yet," he says through grit teeth. And as if proving the Big Boss to the contrary, a tooth comes loose from his jaw and tumbles to the marble floor.

"The process has begun already," Mrtyu says, their tone as simple as if it were a comment on the weather.

I, on the other hand, can only stare at that tooth. He is not above any of us other Reapers. Like us all, he too will crumble to a fine powder, only to be swept into a dustpan by one of the janitorial Reapers.

"Now," Mrytu declares, and a violet light pulses over us four observers. "Would you like to ask your guards to leave so we can perform the review in private?"

"My guards stay!" The Big Boss's fingerbones tremble, and I realize he is afraid. Perhaps he has spent so long forcing an air of immortality upon us, he himself has forgotten the truth. "And you," he directs a finger to the gaseous cloud of Mrytu, "stay right where you are. No funny business." Without taking his eyes off the being, the Big Boss lowers himself back onto his throne.

Mrytu is unbothered by the Big Boss's skepticism, and they

finally find the page they are hunting for within the manilla file. "As you wish, Grim Reaper #105. Shall we get started then?"

I practically see the nervousness crackling in the red embers within the Big Boss's eye sockets, and a part of me almost feels a sort of sympathy for him.

He flicks his wrist at the two outer guards. "Close the door."

The outer guards shift and exchange a look.

"Should we...remain at our post outside?" one ventures to ask.

"Obviously!" the Big Boss snaps, and they both flinch. "Carry on your duties as normal. And not a word of this to anyone, or your skulls will be on the floor." He arcs his finger to the scythe hanging above his throne to drive the point home. "Is that understood?"

"Yes, sir!" the outer guards cry in unison, and with a crisp salute, the door is closed once more.

The Big Boss sets his menacing gaze on me and #2007. "That goes for you two as well."

"Of course," I say, my tone neutral. #2007, on the other hand, only gives a curt, silent nod, and I swear on my corpse rotting somewhere on Earth that I hear him gulp.

The sound of a clearing throat erupts from Mrytu, and I wonder if he's growing impatient with all of this. "Now then, let's get started. Grim Reaper #105, your performance over the past five-hundred years has been abysmal."

A bark of laughter nearly escapes me. I can't help it. But I manage to choke the sound down just in time, and I'm grateful I do not have to worry about hiding any facial expressions.

The Big Boss must be taken aback as well, for he bellows out an "Excuse me?" forceful enough to make Mrytu grow momentarily dim. But they hold their ground and even venture to float a little closer to the Big Boss's throne.

"Five hundred years of servitude, and only one Reaper rehabilitated," the cloud informs us in a deadpan. "One!"

The single word echoes off the marble, and the silence that settles around the Big Boss as it fades into obscurity tells me all I need to know.

"What?" the Big Boss's whisper is harsh, disbelieving. And as Mrtyu ramps themself up to explain, I subtly lean forward and eagerly await the details.

"I understand your training for the position was rather hasty given Grim Reaper #59's sudden crumbling, but that is no excuse for incompetence. Certainly, she shared the basics of the job with you, and Aeon must have gone over the book."

"I have the book right here." The Big Boss is indignant as he points to the Rule Book, bound undoubtedly with human skin. "I assure you, I know every word."

Mrytu flickers with what can only be annoyance. "Not that book. *The* book. The guide. In the library."

The Big Boss remains silent for a moment, and #2007's eye sockets meet mine with an air of confusion. "We do not have a library," the Big Boss says through gritted teeth. The hole made by his newly missing tooth is jarring, and I do my best not to stare. "You must be confused."

It is Mrytu's turn to pause in a stunned silence. Lightning races through their being like the synapses of electricity through a human brain. "That damn Aeon. I knew they were getting too old for the job. So, what you're telling me, is that when #59 crumbled in the middle of your training period, no one from the Branch came to check in?"

"No one," the Big Boss confirms with flippancy. "But I understand the duties of the position. I know what I am doing."

"Clearly, you do not." Mrytu's tone is even, but it's clear that they're annoyed by something much bigger than the Big Boss. "And per Grim Reaper #59's performance review, she wasn't very skilled at the position either. Which means it's been over a thousand years since anyone competent has been in charge of the planet Earth."

"How dare you come into my headquarters, into my office, and call me incompetent!" The Big Boss is on his feet once more, and he storms over to Mrytu with long, meaningful strides. With only a few marble tiles to separate them, something in the air booms, and a shockwave, only visible by the heat it produces, pushes him back a few steps.

"I believe it was you who wished for me to not come any closer to you?" Mrytu points out, and I stare in awe of the power this being possesses. They let out a long sigh, and their gaseous form wiggles a bit, as if shaking a head they don't have. Under his breath, he mutters, "The amount of paperwork this is going to cause me..."

The Big Boss only stares, for once stunned into silence.

Mrytu flares a brilliant purple, then a thick beam of light projects onto the door #2007 and I are flanking. "Shall we go over the Mission Statement of the Reapers to serve as a basis for everything you've done wrong during your reign?"

Mission statement! I step back and study the scrawling, ancient letters. Unreadable to me, but of course they have to mean something. All this time, I never wondered. All this time, I thought of these carvings as nothing more than some relic of the past; uninteresting and unimportant. A spark of fury pulsates at my temples at how complacent I have been.

The Big Boss's jaw opens and closes. No sound. Then, finally, words. "The only mission we have here is to follow our orders and keep the balance of life and death on Earth."

Mrytu dims, and I sense the worry as they speak. "The bare minimum. All these years. And we at the Branch have allowed this to continue for so long, oblivious. Perhaps we don't check in often enough. Perhaps if we had..."

They are speaking more to themself than to any of us. I shift on my feet, leaning in, straining to hear as their words grow quieter.

"I only hope it's not too late to turn this corporation around."

The Big Boss's hearing must be going with his age, for he leans forward and cups his hand around the space where an ear once was, so many centuries ago. "What was that?"

Mrytu brightens, the lightning shooting through their gasses like veins. "Never you mind." The spotlight shines once again on the door. "Since no one has bothered to translate the ancient language for you, I shall bear the responsibility."

The beam of light thins out, and it highlights each archaic symbol as Mrytu reads; first in the mushed syllables of the original, then in the modern words.

"Mission Statement of the Reapers," they read in a voice full of authority. "To balance life and death and prevent the overpopulation of the Planet Earth. To cut the wicks of the human race with dignity and grace. To recover the emotional trappings of the human mind within the Reaper. To restore a Reaper's humanity until they are ready to try again. In killing, we are reminded of what we have taken. In killing, we are shown what we are taking. In killing, so too is the bloodlust killed. In killing, a Reaper is restored. In killing, we are born again."

Silence.

The spotlight goes out. The eternal flames flicker.

The gasses that make up Mrytu expand as if a deep breath has been taken. "Words long forgotten, it seems."

#2007 and I stare at each other. We don't speak. We don't have to. Staring deep into his eye sockets, I can see that we are both thinking of Steven Kelton. Instead of forcing down his humanity, he embraced it. Instead of accepting the system for what it was, he questioned it. Like he was supposed to. All along, he did what he was supposed to do, and he was punished.

The Big Boss is silent, standing statue-still in the middle of the room, the purple light radiating from Mrytu washing his yellowed bones in a sparkling brilliance.

"I was told—" he began, but Mrytu interrupts.

"From what I have gathered here today, it seems your predecessor had an agenda. For what reason, I cannot fathom. Only Grim Reaper #59 could tell us that. You, and all the Reapers she presided over, were fed false information."

The Big Boss tosses his skull with indignance. "If you really are the Regional Manager as you stated, why have you not stepped in before now to set things back into order?"

The brilliance within Mrytu dims with shame. "There are thousands of headquarters located within this galaxy. It is all too easy for some of them to slip under the radar. It is my responsibility to ensure that each and every corporation is running smoothly, and to that end, I have failed. I have nothing to offer but my apologies. I fear now my own progress report will now be as abysmal as yours."

"And who do you answer to?" #2007 pipes up from my left.

The Big Boss turns his fiery glare to him, and #2007 shrinks against the wall, but Mrytu chuckles.

"My own boss is unimportant for the time being. This is a mess I am willing to rectify on my own, perhaps without them ever catching on."

So, Mrytu has a boss as well, and one he also fears from the sound of it. I wonder just how far up this chain of command goes.

The Big Boss crosses his arms. "And just how do you intend to do that?"

Myrtu flares with a cosmic light. "I shall oversee the training of your successor."

Glowering, the Big Boss lowers his chin once more. "I have already told you I have no intention of—"

"You cannot fight the passage of time," Mrytu says. "Like it or not, you are nearing your expiration, as all living creatures in all realms of time and space are apt to do. Now, Grim Reaper #105, either you select your own successor, or I shall do it for you."

Silence swells within the room, and soon the atmosphere feels stifling, like an overinflated balloon, ready to pop. The Big Boss would likely be sweating by now if that were something he could do.

The crushing reality of his own demise must weigh heavily on him, for his entire skeletal frame trembles as he raises his arm and, to my surprise, points a cracked and brittle finger straight at me.

"There is no Reaper I trust more." The words are wrenched out of him like a nerve-wracked love confession. The statement must have been physically painful for him to admit, but it brings on an odd sense of pride within me.

Then, the implication strikes. Like it or not, I have just been chosen to take over the position of Big Boss. Looking to my left, I find #2007 gaping at me. No words come for anyone. The Big Boss still points at me. I suppose he is waiting for some kind of reaction. For now, I simply can't do that.

Mrytu floats closer to me. Although they do not appear to have any optical receptors, I feel I am being carefully looked over.

"Grim Reaper #1632, is it? Let's take a look at your file. I'm sure the clerical Reapers won't mind if I borrow this..." Another manilla file pops into the air before my eyes, occupying the empty space with a suddenness that forces me to take a step back. It falls open, pages flip over on their own accord, and Mrytu mumbles to himself as he reads.

"Let's see, here. Martin Pendergast, death date 1891."

He reads on, but I hear nothing more as the name bounces around in my skull, echoing, repeating, over and over again as an unusual sense of completion fills my being. My name. Of course, I have a name. I would catch myself wondering what it could be from time to time, but they were only passing thoughts. I never intended to find out. I never intended to go as far as Steven Kelton. I accepted my assigned number without a second thought and went on with the course fate laid out before me. But now I know, and now I know how good it feels to have an identity instead of simply a number.

So lost in thought, I only hear snippets from my report as Mrytu reads. "...serial killer...victims torn to shreds...no remorse..."

Who on earth was I? And who am I now, really?

The file snaps shut and forces me out of my musings.

Mrytu's gaseous core puffs up. "Grim Reaper #1632, do you accept the responsibilities of overseeing the progress of the Grim Reapers sent here for rehabilitation? Do you accept the duties of guiding each Reaper toward a second chance at their human life knowing that, as the Big Boss, you will never have that opportunity yourself?"

My jaw flaps. Finally, words come out. "I won't have a chance to go back?"

"That is the downside that comes with the Big Boss position," Mrytu confirms. "Your role is to guide, to teach." They float back toward the Big Boss. Pointedly, they add, "To do better than those who came before you."

The Big Boss lets out a resentful scoff but remains silent.

"Do you accept the responsibilities that come with the position?" Mrytu asks again.

Over the glow, I notice #2007 nod, urging me to accept. Perhaps he has some confidence in me after all.

But if I accept, if I take on this position of great power, then I cannot follow the path of Steven Kelton. I cannot attempt to rectify my own mistakes that led me to this dark, unforgiving place. But is this corporation really so final? I always thought so. We all did. But according to Mrytu, that is not the case.

Is being human again something I even want?

Straightening my shoulders, I scan the glowing being. "I would like to consider the offer."

"Of course!" Mrytu is jovial as he drifts toward the door. "I am more than happy to answer any questions you may have about the position, considering your role model is a poor example." The Big Boss twitches and Mrytu continues, "Shall we take a walk? I can take you to the library, show you the Guide. There, you will gain a true understanding of your role and the goal of every Reaper who comes through."

The Big Boss clears his throat, and I restrain a laugh at the unnecessary gesture. "I would like to see this alleged library," he says, his voice an indication of the authority he is trying so desperately to cling to.

"Me too," #2007 pipes up.

"No," the Big Boss snaps at his underling, who shrinks back. "Check your desk. I am certain there are assignments waiting for you."

"But I have guard duty," #2007 protests.

"You are relieved."

For a moment, #2007 only stares. Then his shoulders hunch, and he edges over to the door. As he pushes it open, he turns his skull to me and mutters, "For the record, I'd much rather serve under you."

I'm shocked. "Despite the...incident?"

He pauses as the door creaks open, then nods. "Deep down, I know you're a good guy. You'll do right by us Reapers. Maybe this place won't be so miserable with you at the helm."

Before I can reply, he steps into the hall and disappears down the long corridor. I'm not sure if Mrytu heard our quiet exchange, but their being crackles with lightning as their cheerful voice fills the room.

"Right, let's go then."

"I would like to keep the other Reapers from seeing you. They would be too curious for my liking," the Big Boss says as he crosses the threshold into the hallway with us. The doorway is so tall, he doesn't need to duck.

"Not a problem." Mrytu drifts to the right. "If the library truly isn't currently in use, we can take the back halls."

The Big Boss only grunts in reply, then turns to the outer guards. "Close the doors and continue with your duties. Let no one into my office until I return and let no one know I have stepped out."

"Yes, sir!" the outer guards shout in unison, and they snap off crisp salutes that appear rehearsed. Loyal until the end, for reasons

I'm sure they don't understand. I wonder if I will have the same privilege.

The Big Boss and I walk side-by-side, staying in stride behind Mrytu as he leads us through a maze of rarely used hallways that feel more like tunnels the deeper we go. I suppose I never stopped to wonder just how big HQ really is, how many unexplored areas there are outside of the cubicles, the break room, the Transportation Room, and the courtroom. I never had any reason to think there might be more to this place. No one has any reason to go anywhere else.

The Big Boss looks down at me as we walk, and his harsh whisper is like the hiss of a snake inside my skull. "I only chose you because I was put on the spot. I still have no intention of giving up my throne."

I look up. Study his weathered, cracked skull. "I, too, fear my own final death."

My words have silenced him. If Mrytu heard, they do not react. I face forward.

"I have a question."

"Yes?" the being's tone is encouraging, and I pause to consider my phrasing.

"If a Reaper were to be rehabilitated, to return to their human life, what happens then?"

"Excellent question." Mrytu sounds pleased to answer. "When the rehabilitation process is complete, the Reaper returns to the moment in time where, as a human, the first murder was committed. If they have truly been rehabilitated, they will not commit the act, therefore starting their life anew from that point on."

"And what of the timeline, then?"

"Time*lines*." Mrytu corrects. "Think of them as threads. The humans actually have quite a good theory for how it works. I believe they call it the Multiverse Theory. It's quite spot on, to be honest. Every decision made results in a new timeline created. If a rehabilitated Reaper chooses not to kill after all, a new timeline is started. Although some slip up further along in their human life and end up killing again. When that happens, yet another timeline branches off, and they will go through the rehabilitation program once again."

"So, there are multiple timelines happening simultaneously right now?" I struggle to wrap my head around this concept, but I recognize that the logic is there.

"Oh, trillions!" Mrytu gives a gleeful chuckle. "Quadrillions! Numbers far beyond your comprehension. Beyond even my own. Quite exciting, no? Why, right alongside us, right now, there is an alternate timeline where the Big Boss here chose another Reaper to replace him. And yet another where he fights me, as he considered doing."

"I considered no such thing," the Big Boss shoots back.

"But in this timeline, you chose not to." Mrytu ignores the Big Boss. "Which was a wise choice. The outcome would have been in your favor. But it's important to remember you cannot do anything to control the outcomes of any other timeline. Best to just focus on the one you're in. Beings all across the galaxy have driven themselves to the brink of madness trying to make sense of it all. Your focus, Grim Reaper #1632, will be to simply guide the Reapers who come here into making the correct choices the next time around."

I nod slowly and struggle to pluck out one of the many questions swirling around in my skull. "So, what you are saying is that all Reaper's will be rehabilitated eventually?"

"Sadly, no." A gush of wind blows past us, rustling mine and the Big Boss's robes. "To be frank, there are some Reapers who simply do not want a second chance. They are content with the fate they've been handed, and they're happy to do their duties as assigned here. Too happy, if you ask me. I'm sure you can think of a few Reapers like that."

Far more than a few, but I keep that quiet. "And how exactly does a Reaper become rehabilitated?"

"You truly do not know?" Mrytu flickers. "Why, haven't you ever wondered about the Random Death Report Sheets? Why you can see every detail of a human's life as you consider making the final cut? Why your memories fade back in over time?"

For a moment, I remain quiet. "I was led to believe that those things were simply the way it was."

"My dear Grim Reaper #1632! Nothing is *simply* any way. There is meaning to everything we do. If you were not taught that, then you truly were failed."

The Big Boss's footsteps grow extra loud in the echoing hallway. "I only passed on what I knew."

"You knew nothing." Mrytu does not appear to be in the mood to indulge the Big Boss's ignorance. "But alas, what's done is done. The only thing we can do now is correct what has been ruined. Is that ideal? No. But at the end of the day, the mission of this Reaper HQ has simply veered off course. I do not anticipate it being too difficult to get things back on track. Especially when new leadership is involved."

Those final words are aimed directly at the Big Boss, and he grunts to show his dissatisfaction. "The library," he insists, impatience growing.

"Yes, yes, right this way." Mrytu is flippant as his floating being rounds a corner then comes to a halt. If not for the gaseous cloud's radiance, the hallway before us would have been pitch black. "When did these lights go out?" They turn the question to the Big Boss, who only shrugs. The gesture makes him appear small, helpless, nothing more than an average Reaper.

"I was unaware there was anything located in this hall," he answers with caution. "I have never ventured this way."

Mrytu must choose not to comment. Their form gives off a little shiver as they mutter, "Going to have to put in a work order to get these lights going again..." With the sound of a clearing throat, they add, "Right, follow me then."

As we walk, I look down at the stone floor, decorated with the dips and grooves that indicate a time of constant, heavy foot traffic. Most of the dips in the stone have filled with a stagnant liquid. This hall was once used frequently. Why did the Reapers stop coming here?

After several minutes of following the purple, ethereal glow, Mrytu comes to a stop outside of a door, outlined only by the thin strip of light at its base. The being condenses then expands with a sudden burst, and the door flies open with a startled cry from the disused hinges.

"This room really hasn't been used in centuries!" The being tuts to themself as they float into the exposed room, lit by the dim glow of eternal flames.

The Big Boss and I remain standing outside the door for a moment, likely both engulfed with a sense of wonder, until a sharp gasp urges us inside.

"What happened here?!" Mrytu cries, zipping between floor-to-ceiling cases of bloated, musty tomes. "They're ruined! Hundreds of thousands of years of collected information, ruined! And after our scribes went through all that trouble to copy the stone tablets onto paper and bind them. So much effort wasted!" Suddenly, the bright purple cloud is hovering right in front of the Big Boss's skull, white lightning streaking in all directions. "How could you allow such a travesty?"

Annoyed, the Big Boss swats at Mrytu like a pesky fly, but his hand goes right through the wispy tendrils of gas, and he recoils, as if shocked. Once recovered, he says, "I remind you that I had no knowledge of this place existing. How can I be responsible if I did not know this was even here?"

The sound of a scoff erupts from Mrytu. "Of course, no one can ever accept blame, can they? Especially those who are supposed to be in charge."

I sense real trouble brewing, and I make a point to loudly clear my throat. "Where has all this water come from in the first place?"

With a quiver, Mrytu lowers down to a normal height, and they appear to take in a cleansing breath. "The River Lethe, I imagine. There must be a leak somewhere. We will have to send in a repair crew. All these books..."

"Lethe?" I stare. "Certainly, you do not mean–"

"Yes, Lethe," Mrytu says. They begin floating around the room once more, perusing the shelves. "It's no surprise considering this office was constructed directly beneath the river, quite convenient for wiping the memories of new Reapers, although the original safety inspections assured us there was plenty of bedrock between the two. Alas, I suppose leaks are bound to happen when proper maintenance isn't carried out."

I turn to the Big Boss, jaw unhinged, but the way his skull is tilted downward tells me that he, too, had no idea our headquarters was located below the mythical river.

"Maintenance will have a field day with this place when I put these work orders in," Mrytu mumbles, still looking through the shelves, searching.

Occasionally, a leather-bound volume is pulled out, and the pages are rifled through with an invisible hand. I watch in fascination, wondering just what kind of knowledge these books hold within their pages.

"Most of these are still in the original language," Mrytu laments as they circle around. "The scribes were in the process of translating when Grim Reaper #59 took over. It appears that business was put to an end." A tsk-ing sound escapes the being. "A shame. I will have to hire new scribes to translate what's still legible into the modern language."

"English?" I ask.

"If that is the language you know, then that is what the words will appear to be for you," Mrytu says as they select another book.

"This one on the number assignments appears to still be relatively intact."

I pause to consider this. "How are the numbers assigned?"

Mrytu is quiet for a moment, as if waiting for the Big Boss to provide an answer. When he doesn't, they let out a loud groan. "You really know nothing!"

"I have nothing to do with number assignments," the Big Boss says defensively. "The clerical Reapers handle such menial tasks."

"I suppose I shouldn't expect you to know how your own branch of the corporation works," Mrytu mutters. At a normal volume, they say, "The numbers are recycled. After four digits, they become too difficult to read on the uniform, so they are only able to reach Grim Reaper #9999."

"Ah, I know her," I say without thinking. "She's quite the killing machine."

"And it will be your responsibility to try and prevent her from continuing to be one, should you choose to accept the role," Mrytu says. The book is gently placed on a wooden table that sits squarely in the middle of the room. A thin, black-bound tome is then pulled from the shelf, and it hovers directly in my line of vision. "And this shall be your guide."

STEVE

The brown spots blooming on the back of my hands have become more prominent over the years, and they catch my attention as I run my fingers over the hardback edition of my latest novel. A romance about a young, witty divorcee who helps her sad sack neighbor get his life back on track. A love story that didn't make it to reality. Fiction will have to do. The back is covered with praise from various journals and lit mags, all referencing the humor and heart within the pages. My latest novel. My best. My last.

I slide it onto my shelf, next to its five predecessors. #3 has a movie deal in the works, but I doubt I'll be around to see it. That's okay, though. I can barely stay awake long enough to finish a movie these days anyway.

As I study the greatest accomplishments I managed to get out of this second chance, blue light flashes behind me. With a humorless chuckle, I turn around.

"Here to escort me to kingdom come, old friend?"

#1632 looks the same as always, although his bones have yellowed. He shakes his head.

"I have news," he announces and motions to the couch. "Sit. You've gotten old."

"Don't I know it." My hand presses against my lower back as I shuffle to the couch and lower my creaking bones down. "How's the old wick doing?"

#1632's skull tilts upward slightly, but my question is ultimately ignored. It's probably a bad sign. He settles on the couch beside me. "I have been chosen as the Big Boss's successor. My inauguration ceremony is tomorrow."

Those are words I never expected to hear, and I let out a bark of a laugh. "No shit? That old asshole is finally passing the torch."

"Not of his own volition. We received a visit from the Regional Manager."

Now I'm really stunned. "The who?"

"There is a lot to catch you up on, Steven Kelton." #1632 shakes his head slowly. "In the end, you did everything right, everything you were supposed to. And no one knew."

I stare, trying to make sense of the words. "Am I going senile? What are you talking about?"

He fills me in, then. About the ethereal being called Mrytu, the corruption caused by Grim Reaper #59, the Big Boss's cluelessness, and the Reaper's Mission Statement. A creed no one knew, no one remembered. A creed I unknowingly lived by. And died by. My head swims with all of this new information.

"So, what you're saying," I begin as the story winds down, "is that the reason headquarters is the way it is now is due to corporate oversight."

"Essentially, yes."

The laughter comes then, long and hard. Giddy, bubbly howls punctuated by sharp gasps of air until my old lungs can't take it anymore, and I wheeze while I struggle to get myself under control.

"How fitting," I say between residual giggles. "How human! This whole time, HQ was essentially just a rehab facility."

#1632 nods, and I get the sense he's amused by my fit. "Things will be different when I take over tomorrow. I will follow the guide. I will be a true leader, and I will put forth the effort to ensure that more Reapers get another chance like you, Steven Kelton. You will be our example. Our goal."

The announcement sobers me. "Don't do that. I'm no one's role model. I didn't do much with my chance. I wrote a few books. Nothing special. Countless people do it."

"Your stories have certainly impacted the lives of the people who read them," #1632 says, admiring the volumes on display.

"I failed Heather."

"She was not yours to save." His chest puffs out, his shoulders straighten. "That's what I came to tell you. She will be my responsibility when she arrives at headquarters. I will be keeping an eye out for her. I will make sure her second chance comes. For you, old friend."

The sentiment warms my heart, and a tension dissolves from my chest, allowing me to sink back into the couch. "I bet the Big Boss is blowing a gasket over all this."

"He was not pleased," #1632 confirms. "When I learned the truth, I told him everything. Now he knows you are still alive."

I squint as I try to imagine the full-blown meltdown that likely ensued. "I would have loved to see his reaction."

#1632 lets out an airy laugh. "I'm afraid Mrytu's revelations have drained the fight from our old boss. You would have been disappointed."

"Damn, not even a gasp of surprise or anything?"

"He's been quiet since the truth was revealed."

"Too bad." With a sigh, I tilt my head back and stare up at the ceiling. "I guess we've all gotten old."

A comfortable silence settles around us, and for a while, we are content to just soak up each other's company.

"Don't you want to know?" #1632 asks as the sunlight in the windows begins to fade.

I lift my head. "Know what?"

"How you were brought back."

I think back to all those decades ago, remembering Heather's desperate expression and the way her shaking hands gripped my scythe.

"Heather cut my head off."

"With your scythe."

"Yes?"

"The scythe is the key." He waits for a reaction. When he gets one, he elaborates. "When a Reaper is deemed ready for their second chance, they must be executed via their own scythe."

I snort back a laugh. "Not the Big Boss's menacing old blade?"

#1632 shakes his head. "That scythe is reserved for rule breakers.

A cut from that scythe is a true means to an end. The Big Boss simply had his own idea of what the rules should be."

"You ever think you'll have to use it on your fellow subordinates?" I ask, smiling wryly.

He stays quiet for a moment. "I hope I never have to."

I hope that for him, too. Sincerely. Reaching out, I give his bony shoulder a pat. "For the record, I think you'll make a great Big Boss."

"I appreciate your vote of confidence."

Slowly, my hand drops back down to my side. "Be honest. My wick. It's time, isn't it?"

His skull tilts up again, the hollowness in his sockets calculating. "Not quite."

I hesitate for a moment, forming the right words in my mind before speaking them aloud. "Why not just do it? I mean, if someone's got to do it anyway, I'd rather it be you. As a friend."

"I refuse to take away the time you have left, Steven Kelton. Perhaps you still have more to do." My heart sinks, and he adds, "But I assure you, when it is time, I will be the one to come to you."

A promise is made. I give my old friend a cheery smile. "Thy will be done."

REAPER #2311

Back in the abandoned library. This time, my scythe accompanies me. It wasn't hard to pull it out of my locker and stride through the halls, pushing past crowds of Reapers heading in the opposite direction. No one questioned me. Hardly any spared me a glance. That's just how it is around here.

The black-bound book is open to its final pages, and I stand in front of the wobbly table and look down at the art depicted on the brittle paper. It appears to be instructions, almost in comic book form. A Reaper hands their scythe to the Big Boss. They bow before them, skull bent low. The Big Boss raises the weapon and arcs it through the air. The Reaper's head is separated from their spine. A blue flash. Only the Big Boss remains.

I dare not approach my Big Boss about this issue, but it seems my scythe is the solution. I'm not totally sure what's going to happen, but anything is better than this. I've made up my mind.

I wonder if it will hurt.

I wonder what's on the other side of that blue flash.

Whatever it is, I'm going to make the best of it.

I can't stay here anymore. I can't do this job anymore. If I'm going to be executed, it'll be on my own terms, by my own hands.

My hands shake as I hike my scythe over my shoulder in the casual manner I so often use to tote it around. But this time, I point the blade inward. Slowly, I pull it forward until the dense bones of my spine stop it. I have to be fast. I have to pull hard. One mistake and I may end up with a half-severed skull.

It's now or never.

I don't need it, but I suck in a long, deep breath anyway.

Grinding my teeth together, I push the scythe back a little, tighten my hold on the staff, and use every last bit of my strength to pull.

The flash is blinding. In invisible force jerks me forward hard enough to rattle to teeth. Suddenly, I am sitting, constrained, strapped tightly to a seat, unable to move, deeply uncomfortable. My vision fades in and out as I look down to find child-sized hands pulling at the straps crossed over my chest. My feet are kicking, screeches erupt from my throat, tears flow down my cheeks and I...

I...

I want ice cream! The big meanie went right past my favorite place! If he won't stop there, I'm just going to go myself!

But this stupid strap won't unbuckle! I scream louder while I pull, because if I scream, maybe I'll be able to get out. And I kick my feet harder, too. Maybe that'll get me out of here.

"I want it!" I yell while I pull. "I want it now!"

Daddy turns around in his seat. His mouth is pointed down like when he's mad at me. "Heather, I said no. Not today."

I'm too mad to make words, so I just pull on the straps again as hard as I can.

Daddy makes a gasping noise, and his hand reaches back to grab me. "Stop that right now!" His voice is loud, but I don't want to stop.

"No!" I scream, and my fingers find the button that makes the seatbelt come off.

Daddy has to twist around to look back at the road, but before I can push down on the button, he yells a bad word. I know it's bad because Mommy put something spicy in my mouth the one time I tried to say it, too. Then, there's a noise, and suddenly, everything is broken.

REAPER #1632

The policy changes at Reaper Headquarters – Planet Earth Division have a ripple effect.

My inauguration took place in the courtroom, stuffed with Reapers who were eager to welcome my new leadership. Many of my fellow coworkers were more than willing to embrace the original plan for this remarkable place. More than I anticipated. Some were not so adaptable to change. I expected as much. I have made it my goal to slowly but surely work more closely with these Reapers.

My physical transformation took some time to get used to. My skeletal frame shot up to twice my normal height once the ceremony was completed, and for quite some time, I often forgot I needed to duck when passing through some of the doorways. The double vision took a lot of time to adjust to as well. Through one eye, I am able to see what is in front of me. Through the other, I am capable of checking in on any Reaper at any time. I try not to use this ability often, as I'd like to think I can trust those under my care to progress on their own. Perhaps I am naïve. Only time will tell.

After Mrytu walked me through the Reaper's Guide, my predecessor gawking over my shoulder the whole time, they left to put in all of the work orders necessary to repair this massive building.

Leaks were fixed. The dripping water remained in the River Lethe where it belonged. Scribes translated and bound the damaged books in the library. The ancient, ruined tomes were placed in a storage facility somewhere outside of HQ – a testament to the long history of the Grim Reapers. An auditorium was discovered amongst the unused halls and was put back into use. Now, those Reapers with a creative flair hold monthly shows for others on their mandatory breaks to enjoy.

Many other areas were also unearthed once the eternal flames were relit by the otherworldly maintenance crew. Classrooms to be used for in-depth training. A music room cluttered with instruments dating all the way back to early civilizations. Recreation rooms with ancient, untouched games that have now been updated with their modern counterparts. Places to relax, rest, recoup, and to take the time to decompress between deaths. As it was meant to be.

No longer are the Reapers simply cogs in the endless machinery of death. There is a purpose here. An end goal. And while not everyone is keen to complete the process of rehabilitation, those that are put their whole hearts into the process. Because it turns out, a heart is not necessarily a physical thing.

I feel I have succeeded in my role every time I take up a Reaper's scythe and send them on their way to their second chance with all of my well wishes. That number is nearing the one-hundred mark now.

But today is special.

Today is special because I have just received the roster of new Reapers waiting for my introduction in the intake room. On that roster is Grim Reaper #7920. Their human name, Heather Franklin. Finally, the time has come. And this time, the plan that Steven Kelton set into place all those decades ago will really come to fruition. I will make sure his final wish is granted, and Heather Franklin will never walk the halls of Reaper HQ again.

The Reapers greet me with waves as I walk down the halls. They are bustling about on business; I am heading for the intake room. The atmosphere has become so cheerful lately, even I have a bounce in my step as I walk. This place is no utopia. I will not kid myself of that. But it is certainly a lot more bearable than it once was. The Reapers here are content, even those who do not wish to make advancements in the program. And really, that's all I can hope for.

I pause outside the intake room to straighten my robes. Out of habit, my hand runs over my skull as if checking for mussed hair. The involuntary action causes me to chuckle. So human are we that even after centuries of living as a skeleton, those old gestures remain.

It is time to greet the newest editions.

Pushing the door open, I step inside and survey the pearly white skulls of our latest members. Three this time. Not bad.

My gaze lingers on Reaper #7920, who watches me with a shroud of confusion blanketing her hunched frame. Of course, for the moment, she has no recollection of who she is. She only knows she is here because she has killed. The details will come later. I can't say the system is perfect, but it's what I have to work with, and I strive to improve it every day.

Stepping to the middle of the room, I clear my nonexistent throat and clasp my hands behind my back. "Good morning to you all," I greet, and their attention is caught. "I am the Big Boss here at Reaper Headquarters – Planet Earth Division. Welcome. We have a lot to accomplish together, so let's get started, shall we?"

ABOUT THE AUTHOR

Sarah McKnight has been writing stories since she could pick up a pencil, and it often got her in trouble during math class. After a brief stint teaching English to unruly middle schoolers in Japan, she decided she wasn't going to put off her dream of becoming a writer any longer and set to work. With several novels available, she hopes to tackle issues such as anxiety, depression, and letting go of the past - with a little humor sprinkled in, too. A St. Louis native, she currently lives in Pennsylvania with her wonderful husband and three cats. You can find her on Twitter @mcknight_writes

OTHER BOOKS BY SARAH MCKNIGHT

AVAILABLE TO READ
ON KINDLE VELLA

The Haunting on Blue Jay Way
Urban Archives

Printed in Great Britain
by Amazon